Cheddar Cheese

"...because the name of the cheese
was unusual."

Cheddar Cheese

by

Francis Lynde

Silver Creek Press

2017

Cheddar Cheese
ISBN: 978-1-945307-04-1 (paperback)
ISBN: 978-1-945307-05-8 (ebook)

Book design by Rodney Schroeter

The Silver Creek Press
PO Box 334
Random Lake WI 53075-0334
rschroeter@silentreels.com

To Doug Ellis

CHAPTER I

THE ROAD TO OBLIVION.

WHEN Barrett awoke he found himself wondering vaguely why he had been dreaming of cheddar cheese. This was the first thought that came elbowing its way through a confusing tangle of other wonderments; as to why he should have a feeling that he had unconscionably overslept, and why his room was so dark, and why the bed was so hard, and, most singular of all, why he had gone to bed with all his clothes on.

It was only gradually, and with the most prodigious mental effort, that he was able to trace out a trail of recollection. If yesterday were Wednesday, then this should be Thursday—very early Thursday morning, since it was still dark. And it was on the Wednesday that President Hawley had sent word that he was to check out of the A to K teller's cage, turning his job over to MacLachlan, and come to the directors' room.

Painfully, and still with the strange muddling of brain cells, he recalled the conversation that had taken place in the privacy of the business room opening out of the president's office.

"Cantrell tells me you've asked for leave of absence to go and get married, Barrett," the president had begun abruptly; and he, Barrett, had admitted the fact.

"The wedding is to take place in Ogden next Tuesday?"

"Yes."

"Cantrell says that you are planning to start West Saturday."

Barrett remembered that he had said he was, and he also remembered that the next question had puzzled him a little at the moment of its asking.

"Have you told anybody when you were leaving?"

Battling strenuously with a half-benumbing lethargy that seemed to be striving to make him go to sleep again, he was still able to recall his answer. He had said that he had wished to leave in the middle of the week—on this very Wednesday—in fact, he had made his arrangements to do so, and had thus told a number of his friends. But at the last moment, Cantrell, the cashier, had told him that he couldn't be spared until Saturday.

Then, as he remembered, the president had handed him the morning paper, in the society column of which there was an announcement of his approaching wedding, with the added item that he was leaving Denver at once for Ogden, the home of the bride.

"One of the friends you confided in must have been a newspaper reporter," the president had said, "and it fits in very nicely. This notice will account plausibly for you if you revert to your original plan and leave on the P. S-W. to-day;" after which had come the surprising and rather unnerving commission.

An important deal for the acquisition by an Eastern syndicate of a certain acreage of oil lands was on in the new Pannikin field, and a large sum of ready cash was needed for the purchase of options from the homesteaders and ranchers. The bank had undertaken to deliver the money on the ground, but under present conditions of widespread lawlessness and crime great care must be exercised.

"The intention was to send Martin with the money next Saturday," the president had explained. "The express company would handle it as far as Araquito, but their insurance rates are practically prohibitory, so we decided to send our own man.

"That was the plan up to this morning; but now we have inside information that somebody in the bank has leaked, and that the plan of sending Martin Saturday is known on the outside. This may mean nothing, but we are not taking any chances. You are going on leave of absence to be married, and this fact is generally known, thanks to your newspaper friend. We trust you, Barrett, and we're going to let you take the cash with you to-day. Are you game for it?"

Recalling it now, as he strove to gather his scattered wits, Barrett found his mouth growing dry again, just as it had when the president had asked him about his gameness. Although not exactly a tenderfoot, in a sense that he was a late importation from the more or less effete East, there had been nothing in his well ordered, bank-clerkly life to fit him for an undertaking which, as it seemed, might very possibly call for qualities not to be acquired in the peaceful environment of a teller's cage. Yet he had contrived to say that he was game.

"If the word has been passed that the transfer is not to be made until Saturday, there will be little risk," President Hawley had assured him. "Everything is in your favor. You are leaving Denver openly, and not on our business, but on your own—so far as anybody will know to the contrary. You will have your ticket through to Ogden, and you need say nothing about stopping off at Araquito until you reach there at ten ten to-night.

"At Araquito you will be met by an auto, with a driver and guards, from the syndicate's headquarters in the field, which are at Drigg's ranch, in the foothills of the Junipers. At the ranch you will deliver the currency to Blanton, the syndicate's agent, taking his receipt for it; after which Blanton will send you back to Araquito in the auto.

"It is not much over a two hour run in each direction with a good car, and you should reach the railroad in time to resume your journey by the Western Express which passes Araquito at three thirty in the morning. Have you written or wired your fiancée when to expect you?"

Barrett remembered saying that he had wired Miss Haynes the day before to the effect that she might look for him on the forenoon train Thursday, and had not yet notified her of any change in that program.

"Well, let it go at that," the president had said. "It will be safer not to wire again, and you can explain when you get there why you are a train later than your promise. We have had just a hint that there may be an organized effort made to waylay this shipment of currency—based, of course, on the Saturday date—and though this may be only some overanxious detective agent's guess, we won't take any chances. You'll be perfectly safe, going so far ahead of the appointed time."

It had all seemed easily feasible; and until he should leave the Flyer at Araquito—without having asked for a stop-over on his through ticket—there need be nothing to excite suspicion. And as it was planned, so had it been carried out—up to that moment in the dining car when things had begun to grow so dim and confused. In giving him his instructions, the president had been particular to caution him against showing any degree of anxiety about the suit case which contained the money; he was to be watchful, of course, but without letting the watchfulness become apparent to his fellow travelers.

Now, this was all very well, before the fact. Barrett saw himself ignoring, with a seasoned traveler's disregard for mere luggage, the suit case which should hold the treasure. But from the moment of train boarding in the Denver station, with two hundred thousand dollars in currency actually in his hands, the sense of responsibility grew and magnified itself until it blotted everything else from his mind and made it impossible for him to take his eyes from the smaller suit case in which, cannily hidden under his dress shirts, lay the tremendous trust. Two hundred thousand dollars!

A dozen times before the call for dinner came—which was shortly after the train had stopped the main range over Plug Pass and was sliding down the grades to the headwaters of the Pannikin—he had tried to pull himself together and shake off the crushing load of anxiety. As a teller, handling every day sums that would be fortunes to most people, money meant nothing to him personally; it was merely so many coins or so many silk fibered paper counters, the total number of which must balance with the check figures at the close of the day's business. But this was in the bank, with the protecting grille of the cage surrounding him and the enveloping and steady aura of the commonplace and the accustomed to make the taking in and paying out a matter of the day's work.

Once, in a record day, he had handled more than half a million dollars through his window, and had been careful for nothing save the accuracy of his count. But now, with considerably less than half of that sum lying in the neat black suit case on the opposite seat of his Pullman section, he was sweating like a ditch digger.

Quite vividly as he followed up the trail of recollection he recalled the problem which had presented itself when the dining car man had come through, droning the first call for dinner. How literally should he take President Hawley's caution about not exhibiting any anxiety as to the safety of his hand baggage? Could he, dared he, leave the black suit case in his section while he went forward to the dining car? The answer was inescapably, no!

But, on the other hand, if he should take it with him, it would be the broadest sort of an advertisement that it contained something that he was afraid to trust out of his sight. There were two of the suit cases; if he should take one and leave the other, the most obtuse of his fellow travelers could hardly fail to put a question mark after the proceeding. And to take them both would be simply farcical.

In perspiring dubiety of mind he had let the first call go unheeded and also the second. Learning by inquiry of the porter that there was no buffet in his sleeper, and therefore no possibility of having the meal served in his section, he had let the problem rock along until the third and last call came. Then he had taken what appeared to be the lesser of the two risks, snatching up the fatal suit case to carry it with him into the dining car.

With the suit case between his feet under the table he was preparing to give his dinner order when the fat man from the section just across from his own, three cars back, came in and was shown to the vacant seat opposite. Barrett had hitherto ignored the fat man, as he had been ignoring everybody and everything but the black suit case ever since the hour of starting from Denver.

And the only thing he noticed now was the fact that the big man was a gross feeder; that he ordered a heavy meal and ate it as one to whom a dinner was a business not to be slighted in any detail. That was all, save a small incident occurring just after his table mate's pie had been served.

"I told you to bring me cheddar cheese with the pie; go back and get it," was the growling command; and Barrett had remarked it only because the name of the cheese was unusual.

From this to the unaccountable fade-out was only a matter of minutes. Barrett remembered ordering a small black coffee, which he swallowed almost at a gulp because he was nervously anxious to get back to his Pullman with the suit case of responsibility. After that he could remember nothing else, save that he had immediately begun to grow stupidly drowsy, and the need for haste or for movement of any kind had slipped stealthily away to lose itself in a limbo of confusion and obscurity.

By the time he had reached this disappearing point in the trail of remembrance he was thoroughly awake and sitting up in the hard bed which, whatever else it might be, was certainly not a Pullman berth. Throwing off the blankets, he put his feet to the floor, and his bewilderment was not lessened when he found that the floor was of rough boards.

Being a moderate smoker—one small cigar after each meal—he had a card of matches in his pocket. Striking one of the little pasteboard flares, he held it up and looked around. What he saw in the brief glimpse afforded by the short, quick burning match appeared to be the interior of a small, solidly constructed log cabin, with a rude stone fireplace at one side and the bunk bed upon which he was sitting built into a corner.

Another match flare added only a few trifling details. One was that there were wood and kindlings in the fireplace laid as if in readiness to be lighted; another, that the single square window in one end of the cabin was boarded up on the inside; and a third was the fact that the place was absolutely bare of furniture or belongings of any sort excepting for a lidless wooden box standing near the closed door.

When the second match sputtered and went out, he got up and groped his way across the room in the dark to the fireplace, a paralyzing fear sending icy chills racing up and down his spine. Kneeling upon the stone hearth, he struck another match and thrust it among the ready laid kindlings. At once the pine knots blazed up, illuminating the little interior to the farthest corner and confirming the glimpses given by the preliminary match flares.

Apart from the roughly built bunk and the box beside the door, the cabin was empty. At least, that was what he thought until he saw the end of one of his suit cases showing dimly in the shadows under the bunk.

With a gasp of relief he sprang up and went to grope under the bed. Both suit cases were there, and when he dragged them out they were still locked, and the locks showed no signs of having been tampered with. But after he found his keys and opened the smaller bag the fire-lighted room suddenly began to whirl in dizzying circles and an iron hand seemed to be clutching at his heart.

His dress shirts were there, just as he had packed them, but the underlying packages of bank bills were gone.

CHAPTER II.

THE JAWS OF THE TRAP.

THE appalling discovery made and verified, Barrett sat on the edge of the pine board bunk with his head in his hands, striving manfully to stop the dizzying whirl of things and get a grip on himself. Normally fairly self-contained and unexcitable, as a bank clerk should be, a rather conventional life had left him peculiarly unfitted to cope with a disaster so utterly blasting as this which had overtaken him.

"My Lord!" he groaned; and again, "My Lord! Robbed! Done out of two hundred thousand dollars, and I can't even guess how they went about it! A drug in the black coffee, I suppose. The bandits must have been in league with the dining car cook or waiter; it couldn't have been done any other way. And yet—"

He got up and staggered across the cabin to the door. It was a heavy slab affair, fastened on the outside. From the door he went to the single window. That, too, was secured, by thick planking nailed across the opening on the inside.

Through a crack between the logs where the mud chinking had fallen out he could see that it was night, and that the stars were shining. Though the month was the wedding month of June, a chill wind sifted through the chink, and by this he knew that his prison cabin must be somewhere in the mountains at a high altitude.

From the window he returned to the bunk bed, opened both suit cases, and went through the contents painstakingly. Aside from the one great loss, nothing had been disturbed. Even the wedding ring in its blue velvet, satin lined jeweler's box, was reposing in the corner where he had buried it in a wrapping of his clean handkerchiefs. And across the foot of the bunk his captors, whoever they might have been, had laid his topcoat, a garment without which nobody travels in the mountain region, even in the heart of summer.

Next he felt in his pockets and was at once assured that there had been no petty robbery of the person. His keys were still on their chain, and his watch was in its proper pocket, though when he took it out he found that it had stopped with the hands marking a few minutes past ten.

This set him thinking upon deductive lines. From past experience he knew that his watch would run for something over thirty-six hours on one winding. Therefore, it had stopped in the forenoon—some forenoon. Therefore, again, since it was now night, the drugged sleep must have lasted for twenty-four hours—or more.

This fresh discovery opened the door to another chilling blast of dismay. The robbery was already more than a full day old and the probabilities were that the bank in Denver had long before this been notified of his failure to keep his appointment with the oil syndicate's messenger at Araquito.

Again the implacable deductions thrust themselves into the foreground. What would President Hawley think? What could he think save that he, James Barrett, had found his price and had proved recreant to his trust? Once more the fire lighted room began to whirl in vertiginous circles and again the iron hand clutched at his heart.

And beyond this? Yes, there was still a deeper depth of misery. Della would know. He had wired her just before leaving Denver, telling her the arriving time in Ogden of the train upon which he might be expected. That arriving time had been 10.15 A.M. of a day that was already of the past.

Unquestionably she had been at the station in Ogden to meet him. Following this, there had doubtless been a hurried telegram from the bank in Denver, asking her or her father if one James Barrett had reached Ogden on the forenoon train. What would they think—Della and hard eyed old Jason Haynes? Della would cling to her trust; to doubt that would be to go mad. But her father—

Barrett recalled the look in the eyes of the grim old prospector mine owner when he had been told that he was about to acquire a son-in-law.

"I don't know, Jimmie," he had said with a little frown wrinkling between the eyes that seldom smiled. "I'd always sort of hoped Dell would pick out a real, for-sure he-man. But I guess it's all right—she's the picker this time—not me."

It had been a rather disquieting blow to Barrett's self-esteem, this remark of the hard bitted old mine owner. But Della herself had salved the hurt.

"Dad just doesn't know you, Jimmie, dear," she had said. "When the time comes, if it ever does come, you'll show him, and everybody else."

Well, the time *had* come, and he had fallen into a hideous trap like a simpleton—like the most idiotic of imbeciles! Robbed without having had a glimmer of suspicion that he was in danger of being robbed and in circumstances that would be practically impossible to explain to anybody's satisfaction; that never could be explained to his complete reinstatement as a man to be trusted and depended upon.

Pursuing the pocket search he drew out his wallet. That, too, was intact, or it seemed to be. His membership card in the Cactus Club, his pass through the gates at the Denver Union Station, his identification card, the various memoranda with which a man's pocketbook is always stuffed, were all there; and in the billfold compartment was his money. Because the wedding was to be followed by a trip through the Yellowstone, he had drawn five hundred dollars from his account in the bank; he had a very clear recollection of the sum, and of the denominations of the bills. There had been two hundred in twenties and three hundred in fifties.

But now, though the sum total was unchanged, the denominations were not the same. There were one hundred dollars in tens, and four one-hundred-dollar bills.

For a moment he could scarcely believe his eyes. Then, in a sudden upflash of revealment, he saw what the robbers had done and why they had done it. As matters now stood; as would be—must be—believed by all who knew the apparent facts; he had disappeared with two hundred thousand dollars of the oil syndicate's money—or rather the bank's money, since the delivery had not been a fact accomplished.

Assuming that the robbers had been successful in taking him and his suit cases from the train without exciting suspicion—and there was every reason to believe that this, too, was a part of a well-constructed plan—the chain of circumstantial evidence against him was complete. The welding of the final link had been in the changing of the bills in his pocketbook. They had taken his five hundred and substituted another drawn from the stolen hoard, so that when, or if, he escaped he would be obliged to use money which—if the bank had kept a record of series and numbers—would at once identify him as the thief.

Hard upon the heels of this terrifying revealment came the conviction that his one slender hope of clearing himself lay in getting his story of the facts told while the charges against him were, as one might say, in a state of suspension— before they should have time to crystallize. A prompt escape from the cabin prison and an equally prompt dash for some town or railroad station from which he could get into quick communication with President Hawley, became the prime necessities. Two full circlings of the clock hands had already been measured since the robbery was committed and every additional hour made matters safer for the robbers and infinitely more perilous for him.

With a blazing pine knot for a torch he turned his attention first to the door. Inasmuch as it opened inward, there was little chance of battering it down from the inside, even if there were anything to batter it with—as there was not.

The small window offered a similar difficulty. The planking with which it was stopped was thick and heavy, and the nails securing it were spikes, driven to the head. Nothing short of a crowbar in determined hands would have sufficed to pry the planks loose—and there was no crowbar nor any substitute therefor.

Next he examined the log walls, but these were even less hopeful than the door and window. Whoever the builder of the cabin might have been, he had built for permanence. The logs were massive and well fitted, notched together at the corners in true pioneer style.

With his penknife Barrett dug out the clay chinking in a few of the most promising cracks, but nothing came of this; a wood rat could scarcely have squeezed through any of the openings thus made. Looking above, he fancied the loft, if he could get into it, might prove less secure. But though there was a scuttle opening in one corner, it was boarded over; and when he climbed upon the bunk bed to test it, he found that this outlet also was nailed up.

There remained only the chimney and the floor. The stone flue, though of ample size for its purpose, was too small to admit the passage of a human body, as he quickly determined; and a tentative sounding of the fireplace walls seemed to indicate that they were too solid to be battered down, even if he had had anything to serve as a ram.

Lastly, he went carefully over the floor in the hope of finding some one of the rough slab planks loose enough to be lifted. But here again the original builder's thoroughness was exemplified. Every plank in the floor was nailed down definitely and solidly.

It was in this survey of the floor that his attention was drawn to the box by the door. Removing the newspaper tucked into it in lieu of a lid, he found the box half filled with provisions; there were two loaves of bread, a glass jar of chipped beef, two cans of tomatoes, one of peaches, a carton of crackers and another of crumbled bran, a small sack of ground coffee and a cooker to brew it in, a can of condensed milk, and a few cubes of sugar. Also, charcoaled on the carton of bran in straggling printed lettering was the legend: "Water in spring under box."

Moving the box, Barrett found a small square hole in the wooden floor filled with a slab of stone. Lifting the stone and holding the torch over the opening, he saw a spring, or rather a shallow well two or three feet deep, with a stream of clear water bubbling in through the stones at one side and out at the other.

Turning the empty box upside down for a seat he sat down to try to start the deduction train in motion again. Why had the robbers been so careful to imprison him, and at the same time taken so much pains to prevent his starving to death?

Either of two answers might serve: first, that they did not care to add murder actual to the other crime; or, second, that they merely wished to gain time in which to escape with their booty. Then he remembered the changed money in his pocketbook and a third answer suggested itself. The robbers *had* planned for delay, but the purpose of it touched him rather than themselves.

They were assuming that, given sufficient time, he would gnaw his way out of the prison cabin, but by that time his unaccounted for absence would fully have established his guilt in the minds of all concerned and his possession of the marked money would immediately convict him.

Notwithstanding the chill night wind blowing through the cracks out of which he had dug the clay chinking, he was sweating profusely when the complete realization of what had been done to him made itself clear. Always providing that the robbers had managed to spirit him off the train without arousing suspicion, the case against him was absolutely flawless. The real robbers needn't figure in it at all, and probably didn't.

The money had been given into his charge and he and it had disappeared together. And every added day and hour of delay would give this most reasonable assumption on the part of his accusers just that much more time in which to erect itself into a conviction that nothing he could later say or do would serve to overthrow.

It was then that the obsession, which was later to develop into something like a monomania, laid hold of him. Since he could never show himself in Denver or in any place where he was known, without the money—since his place in life, his married happiness, and all that was worth living for were at stake—it was solely and singly up to him to recover the huge sum that had been confided to his care; to find out who had stolen it and to get it back, if it had to be done over the dead bodies of those who had invented this devilish plot to ruin him.

Calm second thought, if he had been capable of taking it, might have urged that he was totally unfitted, both by temperament and training, to undertake a task that, lacking even the most shadowy clew, might have made a skilled man hunter hesitate. But obsessions are subject to no law of probabilities or, indeed, of possibilities; and a calamity, so it be shrewd enough, may crack the hardest shell of the conventional and the commonplace.

Be that as it may, it was no mild mannered follower of the civilized conventions who leaped up from the empty provision box and began a fresh circling of the prison cabin. An entirely new set of brain cells was in command, with the mad obsession for its driving power; and it was a very cool, desperate and determined prisoner who resumed search for the weakest spot in the wooden dungeon.

CHAPTER III.

IN WHICH A BIRD TAKES FLIGHT.

FOR a tool with which to break jail, Barrett had nothing but an office man's penknife, a small pearl handled convenience for the waistcoat pocket, but with this he fell to work upon one of the floor boards, meaning to whittle through to the earth beneath and then to tunnel out under the log wall.

Almost at once the handicaps began to materialize. Although he had selected what appeared to be the thinnest of the floor slabs, his progress was scarcely faster than that of a mouse gnawing. The seasoned lumber was hard and the knife was foolishly small and its blades none too sharp. Quite soon, too, he was made to realize that a money handling job does not toughen the hands. In a short time his palms were painfully blistered, and after an hour or more of the whittling he was forced to stop and give his cramped and smarting hands a chance to rest.

Not to waste the recuperative intervals, he ate his first prison meal while he was resting, washing down the dry bread and chipped beef with snow-cold water dipped from the spring. Having missed three meals, he found that he was ravenously hungry; and before it occurred to him that it might be wise to economize in the matter of the provisions, he had devoured over half of one of the bread loaves and made deep inroads upon the small jar of beef.

"Got to let up on that," he muttered, winding a pair of the clean handkerchiefs around his blistered hands preparatory to resuming the attack upon the stubborn floor board. "Heaven only knows how long it's going to take me to gnaw my way out of this trap, and when the food is gone I shall be strictly out of the fight."

During the next few hours of strenuous labor, Barrett, sweating over his whittling job, learned some of the first principles of practical mechanics. One was that a board, thick or thin, cannot be cut straight through with any tool other than a saw; that to make any headway with such an inefficient tool as a penknife, one has to cut a V-shaped kerf, as a woodman chops a log in two with his ax. Another was that a knife blade, when dulled, may be sharpened, after a fashion, at least, by whetting it upon anything harder than the steel—a hearthstone, for example.

Still, his progress was so painfully slow that although he persevered stubbornly the first rays of the rising sun were filtering through the crevices between the logs in the walls before the mouse-gnawing triumphed and a sturdy lift brought out the cut section of the plank. And it was not until he had lighted another of the pasteboard matches to hold it over the aperture thus made in the floor that he discovered that all the hard labor had gone for nothing.

Earth, soft enough to tunnel in, there might be under some other part of the floor, but at the point he had chosen haphazard there was solid rock, the limits of which could not be determined.

At this dismaying discovery the driving power of the obsession began to function with grim energy; he *must* get free and the money *must* be recovered. Otherwise there would be no room on a peopled earth for one James Barrett. Instead of breeding despair the failure acted like the flick of a whip to sharpen his wits and urge him to renewed efforts.

This time he went about it with thoughtful deliberation. Providing himself with a thin stake whittled from a splinter of kindling, he made a slow circuit of the cabin on his hands and knees, and by selecting the larger cracks in the roughly laid floor and using the stake as a sounding rod, he could ascertain in a general way the character of the underlying surface. Before he had made half of the circuit it became evident that the builder, whoever he was, had apparently picked out the rockiest place he could find for the site of his cabin. There were stones everywhere, some of them on the surface, some buried under a few inches of earth; and it was not until he was carefully prodding along the last of the four sides that he found a place where he could push the stake its full length into soft forest mold.

That much determined, he fell to work again with the penknife which, from frequent rubbings on the hearthstone during the night, was beginning to be pretty badly worn. With this additional handicap he had to work slowly, and when at noon he stopped to eat, the second plank was no more than half cut through, and the one remaining blade of the little knife was so nearly worn out as to make a successful finish of the job extremely problematical.

Normally the least profane of men, Barrett swore morosely when he looked at his blistered hands, stretching the cramped fingers and anathematizing the man or men who were responsible. "Damn 'em!" he gritted. "They've ruined me, but I'll hunt 'em down if it takes the remainder of my natural life! And Della—what can she be thinking of me by this time? It's hell!"

Wasting as little time as possible over the dried out bread and smoked beef—he dared not risk trying to open any of the canned stuff with the attenuated knife blade—he fell to work again, chipping, and whittling, wearied now to the keen edge of exhaustion, but stubbornly determined to keep at it until the thick plank should be worn through.

Having to be so careful of the overworked knife, the red rays of the setting sun shining through the cracks in the walls had long disappeared when the thing he had been so cautiously guarding against came to pass. Nervously impatient at the slow headway he was making, he took too deep a cut and the thin knife blade snapped in his hand.

For a time he did not lose courage. The plank was nearly cut in two, and it seemed ridiculous that he should fail with success so nearly won. Loosening one of the smaller hearthstones and using it as a hammer, he beat upon the plank until he was no longer able to put any force into the blows, but all to no purpose. Then he knocked the provision box to pieces, and broke the pieces into kindling fragments, trying to use them as pries to break out the nearly severed square of floor planking.

When this failed, he salvaged the broken knife blade and tried to make a handle for it, inserting it in a split bit of wood and winding it with strips torn from one of the new handkerchiefs. This, too, was a sorry failure, and when it was fully demonstrated he flung himself upon the bunk bed in disheartened weariness to spur the flagging inventive faculty, and, so doing, fell asleep almost immediately.

When he awoke, his watch, which he had set by guess at sunrise, told him that it was past midnight. The short rest and sound sleep had put new vigor into him, and, better still, he sprang afoot with the problem of escape solved; or at least with an offering solution of it so simple and so easily feasible that he swore crabbedly at himself for not having thought of it at first.

Although he had lost his only mechanical tool, there was the fire, the good servant and bad master, still at his command. If he couldn't cut the section of plank out of the floor, he could burn it out—burn the prison cabin as a whole, if needful.

Eagerly he built a pile of the shattered box fragments over the nearly severed plank, and applied the match. Ordinarily it takes a surface fire a long time to eat downward, but now the resinous "fatness" which had made the wood so hard to cut came into play, and in a short while he had the satisfaction of seeing the floor blazing merrily. To provide outlets for the smoke, which presently threatened to stifle him, he knocked out more of the chinking between the logs, and the cold night wind blowing through the cracks gave measurable relief.

Running out of fuel before the plank gave way, he smashed the wooden bunk frame with the hearthstone hammer and so kept the blaze going. In due time enough of the floor was charred and weakened so that the fire was dropping through to the ground beneath. Putting the blaze out with water dipped from the spring, he hammered the charred ends and edges with the stone and so made a hole big enough to provide working space under the foundation log of the cabin wall.

With no better digging implement than the small cooker included with the provisions to serve as a coffee pot, he soon had a hole scooped out large enough to kneel in; and an hour later, breathless and weary, but triumphant, he crawled from beneath the huge foundation log, begrimed, bedraggled and dirty, but free.

Rubbing the sweat of honest toil from his eyes, Barrett looked about him. The stars were still shining brightly overhead, but they were paling in the east to herald the approach of a new day. Although he had been able, the day before, to get some idea of his surroundings by looking out through the cracks between the logs, the wider view showed him that the isolation of the cabin was apparently complete. It was built on a narrow bench of the mountain from which its building trees had been cut, and he saw now that it had been the home of a mining prospector.

In the steep slope of the mountain uprearing itself at a few yards' distance, a cavernous hole marked the mouth of a tunnel, and at the right there was a spoil dump of a bigness to indicate that the builder or builders of the cabin had spent much labor in the tunnel before they had abandoned it.

The first use he made of his liberty was to cross to the mouth of the tunnel. Under its dark portal he struck a match. From all appearances the place had been long forsaken. Much of the tunnel roof had fallen in, and the timbering of the portal was dry-rotting to powder.

At his feet Barrett saw a rusty pick and a worn shovel. The pick was what he had hoped to find. Armed with it, he went around to the front of the cabin and assaulted the padlock fastening of the door; and after he had broken it, he used the pick as a pry and ripped the heavy door from its hinges so that it couldn't be closed again.

With free egress thus provided for, he broke up more of the bunk framing for fuel and made up the fire in the fireplace. Since he hadn't the remotest idea of the location of the isolated mining claim, and couldn't hope to find his way in an unknown wilderness in anything less than broad daylight, breakfast was the first thing to be considered.

Washing the little cooker with which he had dug his way to freedom, he brewed a pot of strong coffee and made a hearty meal on what was left of the crackers and bread and smoked beef, topping it off with the can of peaches which he contrived to open with the pick point.

By the time he had finished the rising sun was beginning to gild the summits of a distant mountain range in the west, and he made ready to start upon his indefinite journey. Repacking the two suit cases, and finding room in the smaller one for the two cans of tomatoes, the crumbled bran, the coffee and the little can of condensed milk, which were all that was left of the supply of provisions, he stood in the open doorway, trying to make up his mind as to the direction to be taken.

With the vast stretch of mostly uninhabited country lying between the two greater mountain ranges—the Rockies in Colorado and the Wasatch in Utah—he had only a train passenger's acquaintance. He knew that the scattered mountain ranges and broad, sagebrush covered valleys alternated all the way across, but that was about all he did know, save that the westbound train from which he had been kidnaped had left the Rockies perhaps a hundred miles to the rear when he had gone from his Pullman into the dining car.

With such a blank in the field of information there was little data upon which to proceed. Once out of the train and into an automobile, he might have been taken far afield; and that he had been so taken was fairly to be inferred from the wild surroundings of the deserted mining claim. Moreover, since the object of the robbers would be to delay his return to civilization until the assumption of his guilt should grow into a conviction, the distance covered was doubtless away from the railroad.

The doorway of the small cabin commanded a magnificent view in all directions but one, but it was not very enlightening. In the foreground the mountain slope fell away to wooded spurs and ravines miles below. Beyond the foothills there was a broad stretch of bare country, reddish in hue under the level rays of the morning sun, and beyond this there were more mountains to lift the horizon to the west, north and east.

Barrett reasoned, quite logically, that the railroad must be somewhere in the reddish colored intervale, and that if he should go straight north he must come to it sooner or later. Accordingly, he took up the laden suit cases, which he had no notion of leaving behind, and began the descent of the slope in front of the cabin, taking for a steering landmark a certain sawtoothed peak in the distant northern mountain range.

All things having conspired thus far to feed the fires of the obsession—that fierce and famished desire to win back to civilization and to begin the search for the robbers and their enormous booty—it did not occur to him to look behind him as he swung away down the slope among the trees.

But even if he had looked, it is doubtful if he would have seen the crouching figure of a man watching him from the farther corner of the deserted cabin, or that he could have guessed what it meant when, from a small box cage under the hand of the crouching man, a bird arose with a quick flapping of its wings to mount in widening circles like a tiny airplane, and presently to be lost in the blue overhead.

CHAPTER IV.

THE JORNADA.

IN a very short time after leaving the cabin on the bench Barrett found himself handsomely lost in the gulches of the lower mountain slopes, and was able to keep his direction only by guessing at the position of the sun. Once among the ravines and cañons, his landmark peak was blotted out, but as the trend of the gulches was always downward and northward, he argued that, sooner or later, the reddish plain must be reached if he kept on descending.

However, making all due allowances for the deceptive eye-measuring of distances in the clear atmosphere of the high altitudes, the descent to the plain was consuming vastly more time than he had thought it would. At noon, when he halted in a deep and shadowy cañon, to break open one of the tomato cans with a sharp stone, and to make a meal on the contents thickened into a cold tomato soup by the addition of some of the crumbled bran, he was still apparently in the heart of the mountain wilderness.

In all the long forenoon of tramping, a march made doubly wearying by the burden of the two suit cases, he had seen nothing to indicate that he was not the first human being to traverse the solitudes. How the robbers had managed to transport him to the lonely cabin which he had now left miles to the rear was an unsolved riddle; but as he went on he had a growing conviction that he had made a fool of himself in his haste; that there must be a road of some sort leading up to the abandoned mine—a road that he had missed because he hadn't had sense enough to look for it.

It was in the hope that he might still be lucky enough to stumble upon this road that he pressed on through the afternoon, quickening his march where the nature of the ground permitted, and fighting off an overpowering fatigue which was gradually benumbing his feet and legs, giving him the feeling that they were nothing but clumsy wooden attachments, and making him swear that if he ever returned to life as it is lived by ordinary human beings he would go into training to make him a little better fit to stand hardship.

It was humiliating to a degree to reflect that he was a man, young and in the pink of health, and was yet unable to take a man's part when he happened to be pushed aside out of the rut of the daily routine.

By letting sheer will power drive the aching and benumbed muscles, he contrived to hobble on until the day was spent and darkness came to make farther progress a mere blind stumbling. By this time he was among the lower foothills, and the cañons and gulches had lost some of their forbidding immensities. Gathering an armful of dry wood, he made a fire and prepared to camp.

There was a little of the coffee left, enough to make another potful, and again he made a meal of canned tomatoes and bran. When night was fully come, bringing with it the chill wind sweeping down from the heights, he was sorry that he had not brought the blankets from the cabin. But with his topcoat for a covering and a good fire at his feet—and with the powerful soporific of utter, fagged out weariness to add its persuasion—he soon fell asleep, and when he awoke another day had dawned and the sun was shining in his face.

So stiff and sore that he could scarcely move, he bestirred himself to revive the camp fire, boiled the coffee grounds left over from supper, and made a tasteless breakfast of bran and condensed milk. Camp broken, and the handicapping suit cases slung upon his aching back, he pushed on, although his pace, for the first mile or so, was little more than a cripple's crawl.

The forenoon was half gone and the sun was high enough to make the lower altitudes he had now reached discomfortingly warm, when he left the last of the foothills behind and came out upon the reddish plain bare of all vegetation save a thin scattering of bunch grass and occasional clumps of sagebrush. Seen thus from its edge, the plain seemed to be well-nigh illimitable, and the mountains bounding it upon the north appeared to be even farther away than when he had seen them from the cabin bench.

But there was nothing for it but to carry on. Somewhere this side of that far-away horizon he must surely come upon the railroad, or at the worst upon some trail that would lead him to human habitations. In any event, he would keep on going until he could go no farther; until the untrained legs, which were growing wooden again, should utterly refuse to obey his will.

The tortures of this day upon the sun-beaten plain were so exquisite that they made the pains of the previous day seem pleasures in comparison. Before the sun was mid-heaven high, his tongue was like a dry stick in his mouth and he was perishing of thirst. Upon leaving the cañons, where there had been trickling streams, or in their absence pools in the hollows of the rocks, he had wondered if there wouldn't likely be a dearth of water in the red-colored plain. But, even so, there was no help for it; he had nothing in which he could carry a water supply, the two tomato cans having been thrown away when they were emptied.

It was of little avail that he cursed his improvidence in throwing away the cans, and cursed it again when he reflected that he might have denied his hunger to save the cans and their refreshing contents for this greater privation. But the regrets got him nothing, and it was now too late to turn back. So he stumbled on, clinging to the encumbering suit cases now more from force of habit than from any considered reluctance to abandon them, shuffling in the red dust, tangling his feet in the sprawling roots of the sage, half-blinded by the sun glare, but developing hour by hour hitherto unsuspected reserves of stubborn persistence that drove him on and on like the whip of a merciless taskmaster.

Some time past noon he stopped long enough to eat what was left of the bran, the sole remnant of his provisions. The dry stuff, eaten without anything to moisten it, went nigh to choking him, but he forced himself to chew and swallow it, well knowing that hunger added to the frightful thirst would soon pull him down.

The scanty meal swallowed, he pushed on again, conscious of little save that the deadly paralysis of fatigue was creeping higher and higher, and having a dim conviction that when it should reach his brain he would be done. But the stubborn will was still in the saddle.

Keeping time to the slogging march, the unbeaten thing in his brain was hammering out a single sentence in monotonous and endless repetition: "It won't get you before night—won't get you before night—won't—get—you—before—night," and under the goadings of the nagging spur he staggered on.

The sun had leveled itself in the west, and the terrific heat of the day was by that much abated, when the first sign of deliverance became visible. With his mountain landmark lost, Barrett had veered and tacked in his course, pulling himself up when he remembered that he must keep on heading north, and falling into the aimless wandering again the moment the purposeful will let go of the steering wheel.

At the sunset instant he happened to be drifting almost due west, and, staring with half blinded eyes at the red disk poised, as it seemed, on the edge of the world, he saw a singular phenomenon. Out of the lower edge of the glowing disk a horizontal slice was bitten, as if the orb were going into an eclipse behind a black wall. When he looked again he saw that the eclipsing thing was not a wall; it was some large object that seemed to be suspended in mid air: he could see the sun's rays under it—on all sides of it.

With the immense weariness dulling his brain it took him a full minute to realize that in this blank wilderness there could be only one object that would seem to be thus suspended between heaven and earth, namely—a railroad water tank elevated upon its stilting framework.

With a cry that the parched tongue stifled into a hoarse gurgle he started to run. Fortunately the life-saving goal was within the limits of what shreds and patches of endurance he still possessed. When he came to it, he found that it marked nothing but a "blind" side-track; there was no station and no pump house. But the huge tank was full to the brim and running over.

Dropping the suit cases in the sand, he held cupped hands under the blessed drippings, lapped them up, and lived again. The water was sweet and cold, and it seemed as if he could never get enough of it. It not only assuaged the horrible thirst; it put new life into him, washing the weariness out of the overstrained muscles and clearing the muddled brain.

It was a disappointment to find that the tank siding was a blind, with not even a pump tender to people it; but even so, there was much to be thankful for. He had survived the desert *jornada,* and in the course of time some train would come along and stop for water.

His thirst satisfied, he began to look around in an effort to identify his surroundings. Thrice during the courtship months he had made the round trip between Denver and Ogden, and always over the same railroad—the Pacific Southwestern. Although he had never paid any particular attention to the scenery—having his mind well filled with sentimental beatitudes just realized or about to be realized—he was quite certain that he didn't recall anything at all familiar in this landscape. Again, the P. S-W. was double tracked in many of the intermountain stretches, and here was only a single track.

It was quite in vain that he sought for some means of identifying the lonely siding. Apart from the water tank, which he found was supplied by a gravity pipe line coming down from the hills to the north, there was only a small, whitewashed corral and a cattle loading chute. It didn't seem possible that he could have reached any other railroad than the P. S-W., and yet the growing sense of total unfamiliarity persisted.

Twilight was fast giving place to dusk when he took another drink of the drippings and walked out to one of the switches connecting the siding with the main track. Out of his Ohio boyhood he dug up the recollection that railroad property, switch locks and such things, frequently bore the name or the initials of the owning corporation. When he fingered the brass padlock which secured the switch and bent to examine it, he found that it was lettered; but the letters were not P. S-W.—they were N. S. L.

It was then that he knew, approximately at least, where he was. The single-tracked railroad was not the P. S-W., or any part of it; it was the Nevada Short Line—a road which, starting at Copah, its junction point with the through line, ran southwest through the Red Desert and Timanyoni Park to its Pacific Coast connection beyond the Hophra Mountains. With his brain now functioning normally, he began to understand.

When he had gone into the dining car, carrying the suit case of responsibility, he remembered that he had known that the next stop would be at Copah. Beyond any question of doubt, it had been at Copah that the robbers had taken him off. How far had they carried him into the region traversed by the Nevada Short Line? This was still a matter of the merest conjecture, but it was now quite certain that the thirsty, reddish colored plain over which he had been wandering was the Red Desert.

With so much fairly obvious, it was clear that Copah was the place at which he must begin the search for clews. Hastily he recalled his recollections of the small but thriving intermountain city. Aside from its importance as a railroad junction point, it was a mining town, now well past the plangent days of the early gold discoveries, to be sure, but still a live and growing center of distribution for the surrounding mining districts.

In such a place it had doubtless been a comparatively easy matter for the robbers to take him from the train—as a sick man in the care of his friends—and this was unquestionably what had been done.

While he was fitting these probabilities together the dusk darkened upon the desert and the stars began to come out. Stumbling back over the crossties to the place where he had left his suit cases, he saw an electric eye glowing far away in the west. A train was coming, and it was headed in the right direction.

Would it stop at the solitary desert water tank and thus give him a chance to board it? He could only wait and see. At the lighting of his last camp fire he had used the final match in the little pasteboard book, so he had no means of signaling.

From the moment when he had first seen the headlight to the time when he began to hear the faint rumbling of the wheels seemed an interminable interval, and while he waited Barrett was of two minds whether to show himself in the path of the headlight and try to wave the train to a stop, or to keep out of sight and take the chance of its stopping for water.

Prudence urged the latter course, and wrote the urging in capital letters. Now that he was about to mix and mingle with human beings again, he must remember that he was a marked man, and that, at the very best, the mere fact of his boarding a train here in the desert under cover of the darkness would be an accusation in itself.

Keeping out of sight behind one of the supporting upright timbers of the water tank, he soon saw that the train was a freight, and that it was slowing for a stop. At this, prudence got busy again. Perhaps he could get aboard without being seen. At least, he might try.

When the long train came to a stand, with the engine fireman climbing to the top of the tender to pull down the water spout, Barrett stole from his hiding place with a grip in each hand and ran down the track toward the caboose. Five cars back from the engine there was an empty box car with its side door standing invitingly open.

Without a moment's hesitation he heaved the suit cases in, one after the other, and climbed up. His major fear was that there might be other ride stealers inside who would dispute his right to join them, but a groping search in both ends of the car proved it to be empty of other occupants.

With nerves on edge, since it was his first hobo experience, Barrett lingered near the open door, ready to jump out and run or to fight for his own safety if any hostile member of the train crew should come along before the wheels began to turn again. But nothing happened. In a few minutes he heard the clang of the up-ending water spout and almost immediately the train started on with a jerk that nearly threw him down.

Cowering in the darkness, he saw the huge bulk of the dripping tank swing past to the rear and heard the clatter of the wheels as they passed over the frogs at the eastern end of the siding. The last stage of the journey was safely begun.

Weary as he was, Barrett had no notion of permitting himself to fall asleep. If he could reach Copah without being recognized as a suspicious character who had boarded a train in the dark at a lonely water tank in the Red Desert, and lose himself, in a manner, in a city however small, there might be some hope of preserving his freedom for the task the pitiless fates had handed him. Wherefore he meant to be fully awake and alert at the moment when the train should reach the Copah yards.

But the task of keeping himself awake threatened to be the last straw. After he had propped himself in a corner of the box car with the larger of the two suit cases up-ended for a seat, he began to realize how thoroughly he was done in. Everything about him—the swaying of the car, the rhythmic clickings of the wheels over the rail joints, the measured drumming of the engine's exhaust—were so many monotonies inviting him to close his eyes and lose himself.

At last, in sheer desperation, he got up and began to pace a staggering sentry-go up and down the length of the empty car. It was in this manner that he wore out the next two hours; tramping until his tired muscles cried out in rebellion; sitting for a while until he found himself nodding; jumping up with a start to resume the sentry-go. It was in the last of the pacing intervals, when he was weaving, leaden-footed, back and forth, that the longed-for relief came.

Pausing to look out at the open side door, he saw the lights of a city on a hill, and a moment later his frayed nerves were set ajangle by the hoarse bellow of the locomotive whistle blown to signal the approach to Copah.

CHAPTER V.

THE PEOPLED AREAS.

FOR a mere amateur in the fine art of hoboing, Barrett made a very creditable escape from the train and the railroad yard when the long freight pulled into Copah. There was no one in sight when he slipped from the box car and picked up the suit cases which he had first dropped to the ground; and the nearest masthead yard light was some distance away.

The train having been pulled in between other long lines of freight cars, he found himself in an alley which had to be traversed lengthwise, unless he were willing to take the risk of crawling under the strings of cars on one hand or the other. Since the most feasible way out of the mechanical labyrinth appeared to be straight ahead, he put a bold face on the matter, and, with amateur's luck, won out of the labyrinth without meeting anybody.

Emerging from the tangle of freight cars, he saw the lights of the passenger station a short distance away, and as he was approaching them a semaphore over the nearby P. S-W. tracks flicked to "clear," and a whistle blast announced the coming of a westbound express on the through line. Again taking counsel of audacity, Barrett quickened his pace, reaching the station platform just as the express rolled in and made its stop.

Pausing only long enough to beat a little of the desert dust from his clothing and shoes, he fell in with the debarking travelers issuing from the opened vestibules, passed out through the station and took the first taxi that offered.

"Where to?" asked the driver, relieving him of the suit cases.

Barrett accounted it one of the mercies that he chanced to know the name of Copah's principal hotel, having once read its advertisement in a railroad guide.

"The Intermountain," he directed, with the promptitude of one who knows precisely where he wishes to go; and a few minutes later a uniformed bellhop was dragging his suit cases from the cab at the hotel entrance.

It was not until he was taking out his pocketbook to pay the taxi fare that Barrett suddenly remembered that he had nothing but the stolen money which had been craftily substituted for his own traveling fund, and it was with a swift qualm of apprehension that he handed the man one of the ten dollar bank notes.

As a moment's reflection would have assured him, he had little to fear from the driver of a night owl cab. The man took the bill, made the change, and accepted his tip with a gruff "Thanks," and Barrett was free to follow his hand luggage into the brightly lighted hotel lobby.

Here, if anywhere, was the place to look for disaster. He knew well the methods of the protective association of which the Denver bank was a member. The two hundred thousand dollars had disappeared somewhere between Denver and Araquito; therefore sharp eyes would be on the watch in every stopping place along the way. If his description had been wired to Copah—

It being Sunday night, there were only a few loungers in the lobby when he entered. His promptness in securing the cab at the railroad station had given him a brief lead over other guests who might be coming from the lately arrived train. Feeling more like an escaped criminal than he had ever thought it possible for a guiltless man to feel, Barrett crossed to the desk and took the pen handed him by the room clerk.

As he was dipping the pen he remembered that to sign "James B. Barrett, Denver," was instantly to invite the lightning stroke. But to save his soul he couldn't think of an acceptable alias on the spur of the moment and was obliged to compromise on the initial "J." with his middle name, "Baxter" for the surname. So it was as "J. Baxter, Chattanooga, Tennessee," that he figured on the hotel register; and when the thing was done and beyond recall he realized that he had now taken the first step in a crooked road that nothing, absolutely nothing, but the recovery of the stolen money, could ever make straight again.

"Glad to know you, Mr. Baxter," said the polite clerk. "This is your first visit to Copah?"

Since it was measurably certain that it was at Copah that the robbers had taken him from the westbound train, Barrett assumed that this visit was his second. But he gave the affirmative that seemed to be expected.

"I've been through on the P. S-W. several times, but this is my first stopover," he qualified. "Can you give me a good room with a bath?"

"We sure can. Like to go up now? Front—show Mr. Baxter to four hundred and six."

EXPECTING momentarily to have somebody step up and tap him on the shoulder, constable-wise, Barrett was only too glad to follow the bellboy to the elevator and to be whisked up to the ten-o'clock at-night desertedness of the fourth floor corridor. Behind the locked and bolted door of room 406 he struggled out of his topcoat and sank heavily into a chair. Now that he had come to the beginning of some attempt to retrieve his misfortune, he realized what a hopeless task he was setting himself.

What did he know about thief catching? And if he had the accomplishments of a Sherlock Holmes, how could he take even the first step without a shadow of a clew to guide him? After all, wasn't it merely a broad guess that he had been taken from the train at Copah?

Then the other thing. Every move he might make would have to be made in the certainty that trained thief catchers were searching for him quite as earnestly as they were searching for the stolen cash. They had doubtless decided long since that when they should find him they would find the money.

That thought about the lapsed time made him glance at an advertising calendar hanging on the wall. In that long ago past in which he had boarded the westbound train in the Denver Union Station it had been Wednesday. Counting up the intervening days on his fingers, he found that it was now Sunday—Sunday night—that was why the town had appeared so unnaturally quiet as the taxi whirled him up from the station.

Sunday—and Tuesday was to have been his wedding day! It wouldn't be, now. It was more than likely that he would be behind the bars in some county jail before Tuesday came around. What would Della say and do? Or, rather, what had she already said and done?

He tried to prefigure her attitude toward such a smashing ruin of everything, but the effort failed. Yet in imagination he could see a little way into the likelihoods. For one thing, she wouldn't sit down and cry, as another woman might.

Besides being the most bewitchingly beautiful of all created things, she was a true daughter of the breezy, self-sufficient West, capable, keen witted, utterly fearless. He could see her eyes widen and the ripe red lips tremble a bit at the first shock, then the pretty lips would stiffen into firm lines suggestive—just the least bit suggestive—of the Jason Haynes grimness. She wouldn't believe her lover was a thief; she'd never believe that.

This conclusion made him feel better—a little better, anyhow. So long as the one altogether lovely and desirable believes in a man, there is hope. Barrett got up stiffly and crossed to the door of the bathroom. The bellboy had snapped the light on, and the white tub and the array of clean towels looked inviting. Having no thought beyond getting clean and tumbling into bed, he took a hot bath and a cold shower.

But when that was done he suddenly discovered that he was ravenously hungry. Rummaging his second suit and clean linen out of the larger suit case, he dressed and descended to the lobby. If the thief catchers were waiting for him, it was no use trying to dodge them eternally; he might as well face them one time as another. At all events, he couldn't lock himself in his room and starve. It wasn't so simple as all that.

Passing through the lobby to the street without meeting any adventure, he went in search of an all night restaurant, and was fortunate enough to find one in the same block. The Sunday night after-movie patrons were comfortably filling the place, but he found a small unoccupied table in a corner, and ordered a meal so bountiful and substantial as to make the waiter look him over curiously—until the questioning look was effaced by a generous tip.

The meal eaten, and the famine edge thus gratefully dulled, Barrett went back to the hotel and up to his room. And since even the sharpest trouble loses something of its point when it meets the impact of a full stomach, he went to bed and fell asleep almost as soon as his head touched the pillow.

Although a bright morning may usually be trusted to bring a lightening of glooms, physical or other, it was with no very cheerful countenance that Barrett turned out after his first night in the well appointed hotel, shaved himself, had his bath, dressed with his customary sedulous care, and sallied forth to begin as he might the struggle to regain his lost foothold in an exacting world.

But now the fine courage which had inspired him while he was whittling with blistered hands at the floor in the mountain cabin, fiercely determined to do or die, seemed to have evaporated with his return to the peopled areas. The task which he had set himself, and which had appeared difficult but not altogether insuperable, when viewed at the distance of the wooded mountain on the farther side of the Red Desert, now took on the aspect of the ridiculous.

Who was he, with his raw ignorance of crime and criminals, to pit himself against the daring bandits who had robbed and kidnaped him with such Machiavellian skill that he had nothing but deductions and wild guesses with which to supply the place of the real facts?

It was with these dispiriting thoughts doing a dizzying merry go round in his brain that he strode across the lobby, looking neither to right nor left, on his way to the breakfast room. Once within the swinging screen doors, and without having felt the dreaded tap on his shoulder, he breathed more freely.

While there were plenty of vacant seats, he saw to his dismay that all of the tables were more or less occupied, and chiefly by men. Although a city bank teller may not have a large out of town acquaintance, Barrett realized suddenly that he did know quite a number of his bank's non-resident customers. Hence there was a chance—a remote one, but still a chance—that he might be seated at a table with some man who might recognize him.

In this dilemma his mind shuttled swiftly. There was a small table for two in a side alcove, with one of the places vacant and the other occupied by a woman who was reading a newspaper. The woman was holding her paper spread in such a way as to conceal her face, but Barrett argued instantly that there was less danger of identification by a woman than by a man. A sign to the head waiter was all that was needed, and a moment later he was seated opposite the newspaper reader.

During the time spent in giving his breakfast order nothing happened. His table companion seemed so deeply interested in her newspaper as not to be aware of the fact that somebody had been placed at her table. Then came the unnerving crash, and Barrett was deeply thankful that there was no heart disease in his family.

For when the young woman put the paper aside he found himself looking straight into a pair of dark eyes widened like saucers—the eyes, namely, of the one altogether lovely and desirable.

For a moment, as was most natural, neither was able to speak. Then, also as was most natural, it was the young woman who first found voice.

"Jimmie!" she breathed. "Or am I dreaming?"

"N-nothing like it," he stammered. "On some accounts I could wish you were. For four days I've been having a pretty horrible dream myself. What brought you here, to Copah?"

"You did," she replied evenly. "But where ever have you been since Wednesday?"

"Where haven't I been!" he murmured brokenly. Then: "I can't tell you here; it's too frightfully public. I—I suppose there is a price on my head."

For answer she handed him the copy of the *Daily Miner* which she had been reading. Although the incident was now four days old, the story of the big robbery was still front page stuff. From what he could gather in glancing over "specials" from Denver and elsewhere the earlier, accounts of the robbery had favored the theory of a bandit conspiracy in which he, James Barrett, had most probably been the victim of a mysterious murder. But public opinion had changed or was changing. If there had been a murder, it was argued that some trace of the body would have been found before this time.

Since no such trace had been found, and the oil syndicate's chauffeur who was waiting for the bank messenger and the money stoutly maintained, and was able to prove by the testimony of eye witnesses, that no one had left the Wednesday night train at Araquito, there was only one other conclusion to be drawn.

James B. Barrett, a trusted employee of the bank, and one who was in a direct line of promotion, had evidently found his price and had proven false to his trust.

This was said to be the reluctant admission of the bank officials, and they were offering a reward of ten thousand dollars for information that would lead to the missing teller's apprehension.

"Now you see why I was shocked stiff and silly at finding you sitting here at my table," said the young woman, taking the newspaper from him and standing it up on the end of the table so that it partly shielded him from the view of the other breakfasters. "I had just been reading that. Haven't you seen any of the papers since Wednesday?"

He shook his head. "I haven't seen or heard anything. You'll know why when I can explain a few things. But you haven't told me what brought you to Copah."

"I said that you did."

"I'm afraid you'll have to show me."

"It was very simple. I met the train at the Ogden station Thursday, and when you didn't appear I found the porter of the Denver through sleeper and talked with him. He remembered you perfectly. I think you must have tipped him pretty liberally. You did? I thought so. He said he missed you somewhere between Saint's Rest and Copah, and thought you had gone forward to the dining car. He was quite positive that he never saw you again."

"But that didn't point particularly to Copah," Barrett interjected.

"No; but something else that he told me did. He said he didn't see you get off here, but he was sure you must have, because when the train had passed Copah he saw that your hand baggage and coat were gone out of the sleeper."

"And then?"

"Then I drove up to daddy's office, and there I found that the Denver bank was telegraphing to ask if you had reached Ogden. Next, we got the afternoon Salt Lake papers, and they had the story of the robbery. Of course I knew then that something dreadful had happened to you—not to your morals, but to you—and I simply *made* daddy bring me here."

Barrett gasped. "Then your father is here, too?"

"He came here with me—yes. He insisted it was just a crazy notion on my part. He still thinks so. Of course, we didn't learn anything new when we got here. Nobody had seen or heard of you. Several people had got off the Wednesday night train, but none of them answered your description. Daddy wanted to go right back home to Ogden yesterday, but I persuaded him to stay over."

"What made you do that?"

"Don't ask me. I don't know. But I just couldn't give up and run away. I *knew* something would turn up if we should stay."

Barrett smiled ruefully.

"Well, something has turned up. I am the something."

The waiter had served the two breakfasts, and though his appetite was gone, Barrett forced himself to eat a little. Halfway through the meal he said:

"Among other things, I've lost my name. I'm registered here as 'J. Baxter, Chattanooga, Tennessee.' "

He was looking straight into the fearless eyes of the young woman as he said it, but there was no flicker of awakening suspicion in them.

"That was perfectly prudent," she said, "and it was awfully lucky that you thought of it."

"It has only postponed the smash for a few minutes," he returned gloomily. "Your father will give me away. Whereabouts is he? Why isn't he here breakfasting with you?"

"Didn't I tell you? Yesterday, when I begged him not to take me back home, he said that if I was determined to stay he'd take a day or so to go and take a look at Blunt Mountain. There has been a new gold strike out there, and there is a good bit of excitement here over it."

"He'd go away and leave you—at a time like this?" Barrett queried.

For a moment the dark eyes opposite were downcast.

"I may as well tell you, first as last, Jimmie, dear. Daddy persists in calling you a—a dude; that was his generation's word for a man who had a proper respect for his hair and linen and finger nails. He says you haven't any red blood in you; that no clerk has: the fact that a clerk is a clerk proves it—otherwise he wouldn't be a clerk. I've tried to make him see that a teller in a good, big bank isn't exactly a clerk, but it's no use. And as for leaving me, he told me I might get on the train and go home, if I got tired of waiting for him."

Barrett nodded. "That isn't all of it," he said. "Go on and say the rest."

"I'm going to—because it can't be helped. Daddy said, right away, as soon as the telegrams began coming from the bank, that I'd had a lucky escape."

"Good Lord! He thinks I'd throw up the chance of marrying you for a paltry two hundred thousand dollars?"

"He—he says every man has his price, and—"

"And I had found and taken mine, I suppose. Well, I can't prove that I haven't—though that is what I came here to try to do. I guess I may as well go to the hotel people and tell them that I lied on the register; that my name is James Baxter Barrett—the man they're looking for."

"Jimmie! Don't say things that make what daddy says of you sound as if it might be true! Hurry and finish your breakfast so we can go somewhere and talk. Can't you see that I'm dying to know what's been happening to you in these four days. You must remember that I don't know a single thing yet, except that you're here."

"I'm through now. I wasn't half as hungry as I thought I was. You go first. If there is a detective waiting in the lobby for me, you needn't be mixed up in it."

"I think I see myself!" she retorted loyally. So it was together that they rose from the alcove table and left the breakfast room.

CHAPTER VI.

WHEN HEARTS ARE TRUMPS.

ONCE more Barrett ran the gantlet of the public lobby, this time with Della beside him. The Hotel Intermountain, being strictly modern, had its parlors on a mezzanine floor, and at this early hour in the day they were empty. Choosing the most retired corner, Barrett wheeled an arm chair out for his companion, and another for himself; but the young woman quickly rearranged them so that she would sit facing the distant elevators while Barrett's back would be turned to them.

"Now, then," she commanded, "begin at the beginning and don't overlook the tiniest, littlest thing!" and Barrett did it, going all the way back to the talk with President Hawley in which he had first been told of the responsibility that was to be loaded upon him, and bringing the story down to the moment of mutual shock and recognition in the hotel breakfast room.

"You poor, poor dear!" she murmured, when he had finished. "To think of you locked up in that mountain cabin blistering your poor hands trying to whittle your way out!"

"That was nothing compared with the tramp across the desert without water," he returned, luxuriating in the bath of sweet sympathy. "Don't you— don't you think the way I stuck it out was just a little bit red-blooded, Della? I hoped you would, you know. I think if your father could have seen me then—"

She brushed the imputation aside airily.

"Daddy doesn't know you—that's all, Jimmie, dear. You are red-blooded enough for me. I think you have been perfectly splendid so far. But we mustn't let it rest at that. The money has simply got to be found."

"That is what I told myself, and it is what kept me going while I was trying to break jail and later while I was making that fearful tramp to the railroad. And it looked then as if it might be barely possible. But now—"

She put out a hand to stop him. "Never mind the 'but now.' It's got to be possible. Please go over that scene in the dining car again—when you drank the black coffee. You said there was a man at table with you and that you noticed him because he ordered cheddar cheese with his pie. Are you sure he didn't get a chance at your coffee after the waiter had served it and when you weren't looking?"

Barrett shook his head.

"Of course, I can't be entirely certain. I wasn't looking for anything suspicious. The man had paid no attention to me all through the dinner, and I'd hardly looked at him. I was thinking all the time of that suit case on the floor between my feet."

"Would you know the man if you should see him again?"

"I'm afraid even that is doubtful. He had the section opposite mine in the Denver-Ogden sleeper, and I suppose I'd been seeing him more or less all afternoon. But I didn't notice him particularly; merely enough to remark that he was big and rather fat and looked a bit like the caricatures of the bloated bondholders you see in the comics."

"Was he in your sleeper all the way over from Denver?"

"I can't be absolutely sure, but I think he was."

"I can't help believing that he was the man or at least one of them," she decided instantly. "Put it this way: when you lost consciousness, he'd naturally be the first one to notice it, wouldn't he?—sitting right there at table with you?"

"Why, I should suppose so—yes."

The young woman pressed a finger on her lip and the dark eyes grew thoughtful.

"I wonder if anybody has thought of questioning the dining car people— the conductor and waiters?" she said.

"I can only guess at that. You'd suppose every member of the train crew would have been questioned and cross-questioned long before this."

"Yes; but they might have missed the dining car. That doesn't run all the way through in the train, does it? Don't they take them on and drop them off as they are needed to serve the meals?"

"They do that on some of the trains, I'm sure. Let's find out what became of *my* dining car."

"*You* can't find out," was the quick reply. "You mustn't show yourself anywhere or to anybody. This is where I come in."

"You?"

"Yes, I. I know some of the railroad people here; the superintendent and his wife and their daughter. I was on a deer hunt up in the Junipers with them last fall. You stay right here and keep out of sight, and I'll go and find out about that dining car."

Barrett protested quickly, and his protest was as emphatic as that of a really red-blooded man might have been.

"I can't have you running into all sorts of things to help me, and I won't!" was the form the protest took. But she merely laughed at him.

"You are just the least bit mid-Victorian, sometimes, Jimmie, darling; don't you know it? I'd do a lot more than just to be your errand boy—or girl—*and that money's got to be found!*"

Barrett put in a rather dismal hour while she was gone. All the manhood in him was up in arms against the idea of letting a woman, and the loved one, of all the women in the world, entangle herself in the web in which a cruel fate had enmeshed him. Then, too, the flaring headlines in the newspaper, no less than the matter under them, were depressing him woefully.

He knew well—nobody better—the pitiless efficiency of the bank protective association of which his own bank was a member. It was unbelievable that he could remain in a Copah hotel for another twelve hours without being detected, identified and arrested. Indeed, it was little short of a miracle that he had escaped thus far.

He was still lamenting his peculiarly hard lot when Della returned with the light of discovery dancing in the dark eyes.

"Good luck!—at least, it's a little good luck," she exclaimed. "Mr. Hogan was in his office at the station and the newspapers had already told him all the things he needed to know; that we were engaged to be married, and all that. So I didn't have to explain, any more than to say that, according to the Pullman porter's story, it seemed possible that you might have left the train here at Copah.

"He said the train crew had been questioned and they didn't know. Then I asked him about the dining car people, and he said that I had more brains than all the rest of them put together, and got busy with the telephone."

"I've known about the brains for a good while," said Barrett with a sober smile. "What happened next?"

"It turned out that the car is here—waiting to be taken on Forty-One to serve luncheon. We couldn't get at the conductor; he was discharged two days ago for grafting. But two of the negro waiters say that a young man was taken suddenly sick in the diner one night last week—they couldn't remember which night it was—and his friend had him taken off here at Copah."

"And the friend was—"

"They muddled over that. One of them said he was a tall man with a black beard, and the other said that the friend was a big man, clean-shaved but for a yellow mustache. But both of the negroes said that they helped lift the sick man off the car after the diner was taken out of the train and side tracked here in the Copah yards."

"And after you had learned all this?"

"It is developing into a very carefully worked out plot, don't you think?" she went on. "I talked quite a long time with Mr. Hogan and it was easy to see that he believes what daddy and everybody else seems to believe—that you took the money.

"He doesn't deny that you might have been the man who was carried out of the diner that night, but he refuses to believe that you were sick, or that you were kidnaped without your knowledge or against your will. He intimated that it was what he called a 'frame-up,' and I could see that while he was trying to make it as easy as he could for me he believes you were the one who did the 'framing.' "

"Played sick and hired somebody to take me off the train?" Barrett queried. "Why should I go about it in such a roundabout way when all I had to do was to walk off?—which is precisely what I was expecting to do at Araquito."

"That is exactly what I argued. But he had his answer ready. He said that you were above the average in intelligence; that you couldn't be a bank teller unless you were—all of which I cheerfully admitted. That being the case, he said, you'd know perfectly well that you couldn't escape with the money and stay escaped—that sooner or later the high class detectives employed by the bank would run you down.

"And when that happened you'd have a perfectly good alibi, and could prove it by the dining car people. And he wound up by saying that I'd better get daddy to take me home; that that was the best place for me just now."

"I think so myself," Barrett agreed dejectedly. "It is a deep laid plot, all right, but I didn't invent it. I'm just the goat. If you stay here the next thing they'll be saying is that you are my accomplice.

"I shall be grabbed; that's a foregone conclusion. The only wonder is that there wasn't a detective waiting for me when I came in last night. And I can't prove a thing in my own favor; I couldn't even be sure of finding the way back to that cabin where they locked me up."

The young woman stood up, and for a moment or two the dark eyes grew darker and then became suspiciously bright.

"Are you really going to give up that way, Jimmie?" she asked. "Is—isn't it in you at all to make a fight for yourself—and—and for me?"

Barrett had thought that a new birth had come for him while he was struggling to make his escape from the cabin on the mountain. But now he knew that those were only the preliminary pangs. As if in some mysterious way, the fine flame of courage and fortitude that never says die leaped from the tense little figure standing before him into his own breast and the transformation was wrought. Springing out of his chair, he crushed her suddenly in his arms.

"I'm not worthy to kiss your feet, Della, dear—much less to marry you!" he said tenderly. "But I think you have put something into me that will make me fight—fight to the last ditch! But you'll have to help—tell me where to begin. I've worn my brain out trying to find the weak place in this wretched plot."

With a little twist that showed how silken strong she was she freed herself and pushed him back into his chair.

"Now you are talking like my own Jimmie again," she said. "I knew it was in you somewhere, if I could only find it. Turn your chair again so you'll have your back to the elevators. I'll keep watch while we talk. Do you think you've got it straight—that the robbers planned to carry you off so that everybody would believe you had stolen the money?"

"I haven't the slightest doubt of it now. Everything points that way. And the plan has succeeded perfectly, thus far. All that is needed to complete it is my arrest and trial and conviction. After that there will never be a shadow of suspicion to fall upon the real thieves."

"But didn't you tell me that President Hawley said there was likely to be an attempt made to rob the bank's regular messenger—which was the reason why he was sending the money by you three days ahead of time?"

"Yes; I gathered from what he said that there was some danger of a holdup, though he didn't go into particulars."

"Well, that ought to give them something to think about, though it probably won't, now they've made up their minds that you are the guilty one. But we need not bother about what they are thinking. The first thing we have to do is to plan some way of keeping you from being recognized and arrested. That part of it won't wait."

"Conceded," Barrett agreed briefly.

"I have a plan, if you'll consent to it."

"I'll do anything you say, even if it is to wear a wig and a false beard."

"Good! That is a promise, and I'm going to hold you to it. You were going to marry me in Ogden to-morrow, weren't you?"

"For pity's sake, don't remind me of that now!" he begged. "Four days ago I was on my way to claim you, and I then had a free man's right to. But now—you are talking with a man who has one foot in the penitentiary, Della girl. Oh, I'll make the fight, as I promised to; but we both know there isn't one chance in a hundred of winning out."

She made a quaint little mouth at him. "It's nice and dear of you to be noble and self-sacrificing, and all that, but I'm not going to let you spoil my plan. Will you marry me to-day—this very morning?"

"Good Lord!" he ejaculated. "Why, Della dear, you don't know what you are saying. Haven't I just told you that I already have one foot in the penitentiary? Would I consent to make you a convict's wife?"

"You are not a convict yet, and I don't mean that you shall be—not if I can help it. Anyway, it wouldn't make any difference to me. If they should take you and try you and sentence you, I should beg the judge to wait just a few minutes until I could find a minister—before he sent you to jail, I mean."

"You darling!" he murmured. "There isn't another like you in all the world! But think a minute. How could it possibly help if we were married?"

"It will help a lot. You are going to be awfully sick, pretty soon, and by noon you won't be able to go down to luncheon; you'll have to have some toast and tea, or something of that sort, taken up to your room. And as long as I stay Della Haynes I can't go near you; they'd turn us both out of the hotel if I should go to your room."

"But what—"

"Wait until I'm through. The first thing and the main thing is for you to keep out of sight, and the only way to do that is to be sick and go to bed. But we'll have to plan together, and I've got to have a right to be with you whenever I want to be. If you can think of any better plan than mine—"

"But your father?"

"Yes; I've thought of him, too. You will remember that I told you he expected to be away two or three days, and that he told me to go home if I got tired of waiting for him. Having said that, he won't hurry back. Are you pretty nearly ready to get sick? We mustn't lose any more time than we can help."

"But see here, you little firebrand," he expostulated; "you couldn't pull a thing like a wedding off without advertising it to the whole world!"

"That is my part of it," she countered serenely. "I have a theory—don't ask me where I got it, because I don't know. It's this: I feel sure that the robbers, or some of them at least, are still here in Copah—and maybe the money is, too.

"They would figure that when you escaped from the mountain cabin you'd make for a railroad, and the railroad would bring you here. Consequently, some of them will be here watching for you—waiting to tip you off to the detectives when the time is ripe; which means that when suspicion has been fully turned upon you by your disappearance. And that time is now."

"Yes, but—"

"Wait," she interposed. "If I am right, our starting point—our only starting point—is here in Copah. If there is a member of the band here watching for your return, he wouldn't betray himself to you, of course. But he might to somebody else: somebody who was watching for *him*. Don't you see?"

Barrett's brain was working normally again, and he began to see the possibilities. If the robbers knew that he had broken out of prison—out of the place where they had taken him—and it was fair to assume that by this time they did know—they would certainly want to know what had become of him.

With suspicion already turned upon him, as evidenced by the offer of the huge reward and the tone the newspapers were taking, it remained only to see him safely behind the bars and their own safety would be secure. And the proceeding she had outlined—the leaving of one of their number to check his return to Copah, and to point him out to the officers of the law—had all the earmarks of probability.

"I see your point," he assented. "But where do we break in?"

"You must leave that part of it to me. But I'll have to have a free hand, and I can't have that if I'm scared stiff every minute for fear you are going to be discovered and arrested. So you see my plan is the only one."

For a long minute Barrett studied the pattern of the carpet at his feet, and when he looked up his smile was a sorrowful grimace.

"Speaking of red blood," he said, "can you think of anything more pusillanimous than for a grown man to play sick and go to bed and let the woman he loves best in all the world go out and take the brunt of things?"

Her laugh was an easing of strains.

"There will be enough red blooded situations in it to go all the way round and lap over before we get that money back," she prophesied. "But you'll do as I say, won't you? You won't make me go down on my knees and beg you to marry me, will you?"

"Not while I'm alive and sane enough to know what I'm doing. But there must be one condition."

"There are not going to be any conditions whatever. But you may name it if it will make you any easier in your mind."

"It is this: if I am taken and tried and convicted, you'll get a divorce. You can do it easily, you know. Conviction of crime is sufficient grounds."

"What good would my promise be when you know I'd break it? But I'll promise, if that is all you want. What did you say your room number is—406? Why, that is right in the same corridor with mine! Now, then, let me see how sick you can look when you try right hard."

CHAPTER VII.

"THE PLAY'S THE THING."

AT ten o'clock on the Monday morning following the loss by the Denver bank of two hundred thousand dollars the Rev. Colby Millen, an athletic and warm hearted young subaltern in the army of the church militant, ran lightly up the broad marble stair to the mezzanine floor in the Hotel Intermountain, hastening to keep an appointment with his bishop, who was stopping over in Copah for a few hours between trains.

In the mezzanine gallery he saw two persons slowly making their way toward the elevators—a man walking with halting steps and a young woman who was apparently supporting and encouraging the stumbler. Instantly sympathetic, the Rev. Millen sprang to offer help, and when the young woman looked up to thank him he was quite dazzled by her beauty; dazzled on one hand and touched on the other by the distress and alarm in the dark eyes lifted to his.

"Oh—thank you so much!" she murmured. "If you'll take his other arm—I'm trying to get him up to his room. A sudden seizure of—of some kind—"

"I quite understand," said the athletic one, slipping a strong arm around the invalid and half carrying him for the few steps still to be traversed. "If you'll ring for the elevator—"

The car came up at once and the stumbling man, who seemed to be quite speechless, was safely gotten into it. The young woman called out the floor, and the further journey to the door of room 406 was made without incident.

At the door the stricken man found his tongue.

"Thank you," he said in a queer, choking voice. "I shall do very well now. I'll go back to bed. I suppose I shouldn't have tried to get up this morning. Don't worry, dear—I'll be all right." This to the young woman.

"Are you sure you don't want me to call the hall man to help you?" she asked solicitously.

"Oh, no; all I need is quiet—and rest. Please don't worry." And he let himself into the room and closed the door.

Left thus in the corridor with the young woman, the ready helper was still gently sympathetic.

"If there is anything I can do?" he offered. "Shall I have the house physician called?"

"Oh—I hope it isn't so serious as that!" was the faltering reply. Then, with a little quavering of the pretty lips: "It's so sad. We were going to be married to-day—this morning, you know." They were walking slowly toward the elevators, and she seemed to be bursting with a desire to confide in somebody. "James—er—I mean Mr. Baxter—wasn't entirely well when he got here yesterday, and now—"

"Are you both strangers in Copah?"

"Mr. Baxter is, but I have friends here; the Hogans—railroad people. Perhaps you may know them."

"Mrs. Hogan and her daughter are members of our church. Do they know you are here and in trouble?"

"Oh, yes—they know I'm here. But they don't know anything yet about Ji—Mr. Baxter. His coming was—er—accidental; I mean it was quite unexpected. We—we didn't intend to be married here and now, but when I saw how much he needed me—needed some one to take care of him—"

"The situation is quite clear," the athletic one broke in warmly. "It is very noble and womanly of you to wish to take your place beside the poor gentleman at a time when he so evidently needs your love and care. There are no obstacles to the marriage, I presume—aside from his untimely illness?"

"No, indeed—none whatever! My father gave his consent a long time ago, and, besides, I'm of legal age."

"I suppose neither of you have been—er—married before?"

"Mercy! I should hope not!"

"Then I see no reason why your joint wish should not be carried out. If Mr.—er—Baxter is in for a long illness—as we'll hope he isn't—it will be very hard for you not to be in a position to wait upon him and care for him."

"That's just it. When you found us in the mezzanine I was going to take him to his room and then go and find Mrs. Hogan and Kate, and see if they wouldn't help me to do all the things that the—the gentleman is supposed to do in such cases."

"Your devotion and loyalty are very heart warming—quite so," declared the young clergyman, to whom pure sentiment was a thing holy and sacred. "I have an engagement with the bishop just at this moment, but in half an hour or so I shall be entirely at your service. I'll meet you anywhere you appoint and go with you to the courthouse to secure the marriage license. Possibly you'd like to call upon Mrs. Hogan and Katherine in the meantime?"

The young woman laid a grateful hand upon the well muscled clerical arm. "You are *so* good and helpful, Mr.—"

"Millen," he supplied—"Colby Millen. I am temporarily in charge of St. Mark's-in-the-Wilderness."

"Thank you again and again. I'll go to the Hogans' at once, and if you wouldn't mind coming there for me—"

"Excellent! I'll call for you within an hour, at the farthest."

They had reached the elevator bay, and he was handing her into the car. As the safety door clanged shut she made one more demand upon him.

"The hotel people," she began, with a diffidence either real or such a faultless imitation as to be indistinguishable from the genuine. "We came here—my father and I—two days ago, and daddy has gone out to the new gold field, and I can't reach him. If you could explain to the hotel manager, without going to too much trouble, just why we should be married so hurriedly while Mr. Baxter is confined to his room—"

"Certainly," was the ready response, "But—er—pardon me, but who shall I say you are?"

"Oh, please forgive me! So many things have happened this morning that I really am quite irresponsible. I'm Della Haynes, of Ogden, Utah."

"Not the daughter of Jason Haynes, the mining magnate, surely?"

She smiled up at him bewitchingly.

"Daddy says I am, and I've never had any reason to doubt him."

"And you say your father knows you are intending to marry this Mr. Baxter?"

"Oh, yes. As I have told you, he gave his consent a good while ago."

The elevator was stopping at the mezzanine floor and, repeating his promise to meet her in an hour or less at the Hogans' house, the young minister got out. Landing on the ground floor, the young woman passed the lobby loungers in swift review.

"Nothing very suspicious looking here," she murmured to herself, and then, walking like a person with a well defined purpose, she passed out to the street and took a taxi for the call at the Hogans'.

At a comfortable mansion in the hill suburb east of the business district she dismissed the cab and went courageously into what she feared might develop into a battle royal. But to her joy, the railroad superintendent's daughter, a rather dashing young woman of athletic mold, was the only member of the family at home. And Miss Hogan had seen the morning paper.

"You poor, poor darling!" was one half of her greeting as Della appeared in the doorway of the morning room, and the other half was a smothering embrace of commiseration. "To think that you'd be coming within an ace of marrying such a poor, weak, miserable wretch as that Barrett! And you thinking him so splendid!"

The young woman with the unreadable dark eyes freed herself gently.

"Do I look exactly like a disconsolate widow, Katie, dear?" she asked, seating herself in the nearest chair.

The daughter of a long line of Ulster patriots looked her visitor over appraisingly.

"You don't; and that's the honest fact, Della, child. I'm hoping you have the proper spirit. If any man thought more of a bagful of dirty money than he did of me—"

"Yes? What would you do, Katie?"

"I'd show him; and I'd show him quick!"

"That, my dear Katherine, is precisely what I'm planning to do—and I hope you and your mother are not going to think it's too horribly callous of me. Did I ever tell you anything about Jimmie Baxter?"

"Not the first word. Who might he be?"

"He is a man I met when I was East in school. He fell in love with me then—or he says he did; anyway, he wanted to marry me when I was graduated. But I wasn't ready then."

"Of course you weren't! And then this Barrett scalawag came butting in and—"

"Wait, Katie, dear; you haven't heard it all. The most wonderful thing has happened. While I was at breakfast in the hotel this morning somebody came and sat down opposite me. I nearly fainted when I saw it was Jimmie Baxter. He was traveling for somebody or—or something, and it just happened; our meeting that way, I mean."

"Well?"

"Katie, he loves me just as much as ever he did. He has read the papers and he knows what an awful thing has happened to me. He is one of God's own gentlemen, Katie, dear. What do you suppose he wants me to do?"

"I know well enough what I'd want you to do if I were a man and stood in his shoes. I'd make you marry me, whether you wanted to or no! Then you could show the world and all that you're not breaking your heart over a man that couldn't even keep faith with his job—let alone with a woman."

"Oh! Do you really think people would believe that I didn't care?" This in wide-eyed innocency that would have deceived the most astute of inquisitors.

"Wouldn't you be giving them the best proof in the world that you didn't? But is this new man really in earnest? Or is he just swept off his feet, like, by this trouble that's come to you?"

"Yes, dear; he is in earnest; but maybe I'm the one that's swept off. He is willing to wait and have a church wedding and all that, but I'm not willing to wait. He was looking awfully bad when I met him, and he ate almost no breakfast at all. And, just a little while after we talked, he had to go back to bed in his room at the hotel. Mr. Millen, of St. Mark's, helped me take poor Jimmie up from the parlors to his floor. Katie, dear, I want the right to go and take care of him—and I want it *now!*"

"But, Della, child—if he is sick—"

"Isn't that all the more reason? Mr. Millen seems to think it is. He is coming here presently to go with me to get the license. And I want you and your mother for witnesses—just you two, you know. Of course, the way things are, it must be very quiet and unexciting; just as simple as we can make it."

At this conjuncture it was the resolute Miss Hogan who was in danger of being swept off her feet.

"You'd do this, Della—without waiting for your father to come back, or anything? I'm thinking that butter wouldn't melt in your mouth, dear; that's what I'm thinking. Why, you sly little witch, you had this party all spoken for before ever you came here, even to putting the comether on Colby Millen! We'll come—mother and I; sure we'll come—only you don't need us at all. Anybody would do for witnesses."

"Oh, yes; I do need you both. You are the only friends I have in Copah, and you know everybody that is anybody. I don't care any more for the conventions than I have to, but I—I really should love to have people get this thing right. You know what I mean. I'd like to have people know that I *have* the proper spirit, as you put it; that I wasn't obliged to be left a waiting bride at the altar to-morrow. You see what I'm trying to say."

"I see," was the sisterly rejoinder, "and I'm *crying* proud of you, Della, dear. And we'll take good care that other people see, too. I only hope you'll be as happy as you deserve to be."

"Don't worry about that. I've never been so sure of myself as I am this morning. Now if Mr. Millen would come—"

"He's coming up the walk this minute," said the large hearted one, looking out of the window. Then, going swiftly into action: "You meet him and go with him, dear, whilst I run upstairs and get some clothes on me. Mother's gone to the hospital to see a sick woman, but I'll take the roadster and pick her up. We'll meet you at the hotel by the time you're ready."

Quite as self-possessed as if she had been the hostess instead of a visitor, Miss Haynes met the young minister at the door.

"I am ready," she said with a smile that no man, old or young, could have withstood. "Miss Hogan asks to be excused. She is preparing to go after her mother, who is out, and they'll both meet us at the hotel."

"Very good. You don't mind walking? I'm not rich enough to own a car."

Secretly, in her heart, Della promised herself that this sympathetic young laborer in the vineyard, who looked so much more like a football athlete than a minister, should later have a car, if she had to buy it out of her dowry. But aloud she said: "I like to walk. I've tramped all day long after deer or bear in the Junipers and I love it."

There was not much said on the walk of a few squares to the courthouse, but the Rev. Millen, who was as conscientious as he was sympathetic, was doing a goodly lot of thinking. The young woman's giving of her name at the last moment in the hotel elevator had proved a rather shocking revealment.

He had read the newspapers and, like everybody else within reach of the Associated Press specials, he knew that the absconding bank teller, Barrett, was engaged to be married to the daughter of Jason Haynes, the wealthy mine owner of Utah—was, in fact, on his way to his wedding when he yielded to the base temptation.

Most naturally, Millen accepted the only conclusion that offered: Miss Haynes, mortified and humiliated by the position in which she found herself, had accidentally met an old flame at the breakfast table in the hotel, and had permitted herself to be caught in the rebound, angry pride adding its flick of the whiplash. True, she had not gone into the details with him, but he was wise enough in the ways of men and maidens to be able to piece out the story for himself.

Summing it up, it presented a case in which his duty as a man and a minister was clear. So when they entered the courthouse, he drew her to a seat on a bench in the rotunda and sat down beside her.

"I must talk with you a few minutes before you take the final step, Miss Haynes," he began gravely. "And first I must ask a few questions, which I hope you will answer frankly and freely. Is it not true that you were engaged to this man, Barrett, who, as it seems, has robbed his employers?"

She nodded brightly. "Yes; it is true."

"And, but for this despicable thing he has done, you would have married him?"

"I suppose I should."

"Pardon me if my duty makes me break down all the barriers, Miss Haynes, but—did you love this man?"

"I—I thought I did."

"But now you are going to marry another man on the spur of the moment. My dear young lady, I am asking you to think well before you take this irrevocable step. I want you to ask yourself, honestly and fairly, if, in marrying this sick man, you are not doing yourself and him a cruel injustice; if you are not moved to take this step more because of wounded pride and a natural—a very natural—desire to show the world that your heart was not touched, than for any real feeling of love that you have for Mr. Baxter."

Her reply was prompt and apparently unequivocal.

"I know very well what I am doing, Mr. Millen, and my conscience is perfectly at ease. Whatever has happened in the past I am sure of this: that I love the man you helped me take to his room in the hotel a little while ago with all my heart, and there is no sacrifice too great for me to make for him. I know what you will say, and what the world will say—for a little while, at least—that I was caught in the rebound; that I married in a fit of pique, and to try to make people believe that I didn't care.

"Let it be so. Believe it if you wish; and if others ask you about it you may say that I didn't deny it when you asked me if it were so. Is there anything else you would like to know? If not, wouldn't we better get through with the formalities? I don't want to keep Mrs. Hogan and Katherine waiting."

The young minister sighed and gave it up. There was a touch of defiance in her tone to warn him that he had gone as far as he dared—if not a little too far. Apparently there was no obstacle, legal or ecclesiastical, in which case he could only do his office and hope for the best.

At the official desk to which he led her he explained the circumstances in which the bride, and not the groom, was applying for the license, and was somewhat relieved at the readiness with which his companion answered all the questions that were put to her about the groom's age, his birthplace, nativity, and so on.

It argued that she was not marrying a stranger, at all events. Also, it argued well that she was not in the least embarrassed, save when it came to giving the names.

"Is it absolutely necessary that you should have the full names?" she asked; and when the clerk said that it was customary, she asked again: "Wouldn't the marriage be legal unless the full names were given?"

The license clerk was no lawyer and he confessed it smilingly and passed the query over to the clergyman. "How about that, Mr. Millen?" he inquired.

But here it was a case of the blind leading the blind.

"I don't know how the law regards it; the church deals only with the Christian names: 'Do you, James, take this woman, Della,' and so forth."

"I guess we have names enough," said the clerk, and it was to James Baxter and Della Haynes that the license was made out.

On the short walk around to the hotel the young minister thought of something else.

"Do you—er—want the ring ceremony, Miss Della?" he asked.

"Why—yes," she returned; "it ought to be, oughtn't it?"

"If you wish it, certainly. Have you a ring that will answer?"

"I haven't, but I'll get one," was the prompt reply; whereupon she steered him into a jeweler's shop and let him wait while she chose a plain gold band, calmly fitting it upon the third finger of her left hand and removing, as Millen noticed, a very beautiful diamond in a platinum setting to permit the fitting.

He gasped a bit at this. The diamond, he argued, must be the Barrett engagement ring. And he was relieved when she didn't put it on again; when she dropped it into her purse with the gold band and signified her readiness to go.

In the hotel parlors they found Mrs. Hogan and her daughter waiting, the younger woman with her Irish eyes sparkling, and the older looking a trifle dubious, but with her lips set as if she were firmly determined to see this most unconventional proceeding on the part of the younger generation through to a respectable end.

Two minutes later the young minister, heading the party of four, was tapping at the door of room 406 in the fourth floor corridor, bending his head to listen for the permission to enter.

CHAPTER VIII.

FOR BETTER OR WORSE.

OBEDIENT to orders, Barrett had gone honestly to bed after the retreat to his room, so it was a rather wan looking young man in pink pyjamas who, from his propping of pillows, greeted the wedding party as it filed solemnly into the room. Della was the first to reach his bedside.

"Play up, Jimmie, dear—for pity's sake!" she whispered hurriedly; and then: "I've got a ring; don't forget and try to find your own!"

"So dear of you to be willing to tie yourself to a sick man," he said, loud enough so the others could hear; but his kiss, when he drew her down to him, had nothing of the stage quality in it.

Very gently she disengaged herself and with exactly the proper shade of bridely embarrassment introduced him to Mrs. Hogan, to Kate, and to Millen. Barrett's fine resolves became as water in his bones. Again and again during the interval of waiting he had sternly determined to make a clean breast of everything when Della should appear with the minister; to do this and firmly to forbid the sacrifice—an attitude in which he felt sure any minister of the Gospel would support him.

But the presence of the two women witnesses was an insurmountable obstacle. He knew women—a little—or thought he did, and he was well convinced that a confession of his real identity before Mrs. Hogan and her daughter would be equivalent to crying it from the housetops. With a faint groan he acknowledged the introductions; then the clergyman drew his little black book from an inner pocket, and a moment later his chancel voice was filling the room: "Dearly beloved, we are gathered together here—"

As all the world knows, the Episcopal marriage ceremony is mercifully short. Della's responses were clear and distinct, and Barrett's—well, they were as hearty as a sick man could be expected to make. At the question, "Who giveth this woman to be married to this man?" Mrs. Hogan felt that something was incumbent upon her, so she said, quite majestically: "I do," and then followed the solemn troth plighting and the ceremony of the ring, the prayers, the joining of hands; after which, with his brain in a whirl, Barrett heard, as from a great distance, the irrevocable pronouncement: "Forasmuch as James and Della have consented together in holy wedlock—and thereto have given and pledged their troth—I pronounce that they are man and wife—"

It was not until it was all over and Kate Hogan was smothering the bride in an athletic embrace, that Barrett remembered that his money—all the money he had—was accursed. Choking with dismay, he held out his arms to his wife and while he held her close it was no sweet endearment that passed between them.

Barrett's hoarse whisper was: "Money—have you got any money for the—the fee?"

"Plenty of it," she whispered back.

"Thank Heaven!" he gasped. "My pocketbook is under the pillows; take it out, but don't give him any of that money: I'll explain later."

"Trust me," she breathed; and in a few minutes the formalities were complied with, the door closed upon the forger of happy shackles and his two accomplices, and husband and wife were alone together.

Barrett sat up in bed and put his face in his hands.

"Della, dear," he began hoarsely, "if I don't win out of this with a clean slate I'll make you a widow in sober fact; I'll promise you that! I feel like a yellow dog!"

She gave him a smile that, under less harrowing conditions, would have set him afire.

"Is that the way it makes you feel to be married to me?" she mocked. Then:

"It's about luncheon time. Are you hungry?"

"Just at the present moment I am a good many things that you will never understand; but I suppose even a yellow dog may have an appetite. How are you going to feed me?"

"I'll show you pretty soon. I'm going down to luncheon now and to face whatever curiosity there may be below stairs. The hotel people know we are married. Mr. Millen told them we were going to be."

"Can't we have luncheon sent up here and eat it together?"

"We could, but we're not going to. It is my part to spy out the land and I can't do it if I stay here with you. We mustn't forget that this little one-act piece of a wedding we've staged for the benefit of Mrs. Grundy is only the curtain raiser for the real thing. We've got to find those bandits and get that money back. And time is awfully precious."

It had been Barrett's invariable rule never to smoke before meals, but at the moment he felt that a sedative of some kind was a crying necessity.

"If you'll feel in my coat pocket over there and get me a cigar before you go," he begged. "You may not believe it, but I'm all nerves. I want to get up and fight somebody. This hiding out business is simply dastardly!"

"Woof!" she said with a little imitation shudder. "I like you when you look all savage and fierce like that. It makes me want to rumple your hair and say, sic 'em!—only the pink pyjamas do take the edge off a little. Whoever told you you ought to buy pink pyjamas, Jimmie, dear?" But she got him the cigar and held a match for him to light it before she vanished.

Left to himself, Barrett sank back among the pillows to blow reflective smoke rings at the ceiling. The kaleidoscopic whirl of things in the past few hours had left him in a daze from which he was just beginning to emerge. How completely and hopelessly an orderly and moderately well behaved world had been turned topsy-turvy for him in a few short days! Would he ever be able to win back to things normal and conventional again?

What had the revolutionary fate that had laid hold of him and jerked him out of his accustomed and comfortable rut still in store for him? Would the cloud of guilt that enveloped him be cleared away so that he could once more take his place behind the bronze window grille in the bank? Or would the slender thread of a chance that Della—God bless her! was trying to spin, break and drop him into a prison cell?

Dubious as the outlook was, a thrill of joy ran tingling to his finger tips when he realized, as he might never have realized in the ordinary, conventional run of things, to what superb heights a woman's love and loyalty could rise. Della knew; she believed in him; she would fight for him. Heavens, what a treasure he had found and plucked out of the ghastly tangle of things!

"She knows perfectly well that I haven't a Chinaman's chance of keeping out of prison," he told himself, "but she was determined to make the last glorious sacrifice of herself while there was yet time. God, how I love her and the very ground she walks on! And if the Chinaman's chance should happen to come my way, I'll fight and die before I'll let her sweet life be spoiled!"

Wherein, little as he might appreciate or apprehend it, spoke a very different sort of man from the James Barrett of the teller's cage; the James Barrett whom the Denver haberdashers knew as a difficult customer when it came to the nice and important matter of matching colors in socks and neckties.

The better part of an hour had slipped away before a stir in the corridor warned him that the curtain was about to rise upon another act. But when the door was opened it was only to admit Della, carrying a tray upon which was disposed a sick man's luncheon; namely, a pot of tea and a stack of buttered toast under a napkin.

"Don't swear," she begged, when she put the tray down and came to beat up his pillows. "I couldn't let you get well and all wolfishly hungry in too big a hurry, you know. It wouldn't look reasonable. But I'll smuggle you up something substantial for dinner this evening if I have to buy it at a restaurant and bring it in under my arm. Did you think I was never coming back?"

"I thought, and I am always going to think, that every minute I spend away from you is a minute lost, ruined, blacked out of my life. And as for the toast and tea—'Better is a dinner of herbs where love is—' "

" 'Than a stalled ox and hatred therewith,' " she finished, laughing. "Only there is hatred, too, of a sort, only it hasn't yet got above the ground floor, thanks be. Eat your toast and I'll tell you what I've found out. But tell me first, how many people know your middle name?"

"I think you are the only person this side of Ohio who knows it. Why?"

"Are you quite sure nobody in Denver knows it?"

"Reasonably sure. I've never used it—never liked it. It's the name of an uncle by marriage on my mother's side, and I have always cordially detested the uncle."

"So far, so good. As I was passing through the lobby on my way to the dining room a little while ago, a man came from the street and went to the registry desk. Do you believe in intuition and such things?"

"I'll believe in anything you lay claim to. Go on."

"I had what daddy would call a 'hunch' right away; I don't know why, because the man didn't look like a Sherlock Holmes or anything of that sort. I made believe I was looking for a magazine, and so killed time at the newsstand until he got through talking to the registry clerk and went away. Then I went across to the desk and fascinated the clerk. You didn't know I could fascinate people when I try, did you?"

"The man is a detective?" Barrett asked; and he found the toast growing dry in his mouth.

"The hotel people think he is. He has been here for two days, watching the register and asking questions about all the new names: yours was one of them that he asked about. The clerk very obligingly told him that you came in on the late train last night, that you were sick in bed and that you'd just married me."

Barrett groaned. "If he is any kind of a sleuth at all he won't be satisfied with any such sketch as that. The next thing we know, he'll be trying to break in here and get a sight of me. And then it will be all over but notifying the undertaker."

The bride of an hour was sitting on the edge of the bed, elbows on knees and her face propped in the cup of her hands.

"If we could only disguise you in some way," she mused. "If he is really suspicious, he'll bribe the corridor man or the chambermaid, or somebody, and get his chance to look at you. Did you ever wear a beard and mustache, Jimmie?"

"Never!" said Barrett fervently, having come upon the mundane scene some years after beards had been banished from the faces of all men.

"But you would wear them—for my sake—wouldn't you?"

"I'd grow a pig's nose if you wanted me to. But, dearest, a man can't raise a beard and a mustache while you wait."

"Never mind. We'll keep the door locked this afternoon, anyway. Now I have some news of another kind. What would you say if I should tell you that I think I have found one of the robbers?"

"Oh, but you couldn't; when you don't know any more than I do who they are."

"Still, I believe I have found one of them. Let's go back to that dinner in the dining car. You said that the man who sat opposite you was a big man: was he red-faced?"

Barrett tried to remember. "Yes; I think he was."

"And with a little bald spot at the crown of his head?"

"I can't say; I didn't notice the crown of his head."

"Smoothed-shaved?"

"No; he wore a mustache, heavy and blond."

"Exactly. When I went into the dining room a little while ago I looked all around, wondering if one of them mightn't be there, watching and waiting for you to turn up. There wasn't anybody that looked at all suspicious; even a big man with a red face, a blond mustache and a little round bald spot didn't look suspicious.

"But when my eyes fell upon him I had another of those queer little mental elbowings, so I had the waiter put me at a table where I could see him as I ate. He was alone and he didn't say or do anything out of the usual until just at the very last, when the waiter brought his pie."

"And then," said Barrett tragically, starting up in bed, "then he told the waiter to take the cheese back and bring him cheddar!"

"That, Jimmie, dear, is precisely what he did. I nearly choked over my tea when I heard him say, growling like a bear: 'Cheddar, *cheddar!* I told you to bring me *cheddar* cheese, didn't I?' It fairly took my breath away."

"You didn't let it rest at that?" Barrett broke in eagerly.

"You may believe I didn't. After luncheon, while the kitchen people were getting your toast and tea ready, I had another little talk with the registry clerk. He's a nice young man, Jimmie. I believe he'd tell me the inmost secrets of his heart if I should ask him.

"That big man who is so fond of cheddar cheese has been here since last Thursday morning. He claims to be interested in mines and says he is waiting for somebody who is to meet him here. You'll say there is no proof that he is the robber, or one of them, which is perfectly true.

"But, just the same, *he is the man who could tell what became of you after you lost consciousness in the diner!* And not only of you, but of the suit case you had on the floor between your feet."

"It would be absolutely incredible—but for the cheese," Barrett protested.

"But that part of it does seem to ring the bell. If I could have a few minutes alone with this cheese epicure I'd make him tell me a few things—or I'd sweat some of the fat off him trying!"

Della ran soothing fingers through his hair.

"Easy does it, dear," she cautioned. "Leave it to me, and I'll find out all the things we need to know. It's the detective that is bothering me most just now. We've got to get rid of him in some way. And we've got to work fast.

"It is plain enough to me that the big man is waiting in the expectation that you will turn up here in Copah, so he can point you out to the officers. But he won't wait indefinitely. Besides, daddy will be back sometime; and we don't need any more complications than we have now."

"Ump!" said Barrett, sipping the hot tea. "You certainly said a generous mouthful then. Your father will murder me and any jury that was ever impaneled would acquit him—and very properly, too. How long have I got to stay in bed?"

"You mustn't be impatient. Bed is the safest place for you right now. It's a mercy you disappeared from the public gaze as promptly as you did this morning. With two men stopping here in the hotel, both of them on the lookout for you—"

"But you can't imagine how it grinds me to stay here and hide behind your skirts, Della! If, by some unheard of fluke, we should happen to win and get the money back your father will never forgive me for this part of it."

"Never mind daddy," she returned lightly. "Results are what count with him. And, speaking of money, what is the matter with the money you've got in that fat pocketbook under your pillows? I'm asking because we'll probably have to use some of it before we're through."

"It's counterfeit money, so far as any use we can make of it is concerned," he told her; and then he explained the trap the robbers had set for him by the exchange of bank notes.

"What do you know about that!" she exclaimed. "Have you spent any of it?"

"I had to pay the taxi driver who brought me up from the railroad station last night. The only good money I have is the change he gave me out of a ten dollar bill. I didn't remember, until after I was in for it, that I didn't have any money that was safe to spend."

"Luckily, you've married ready money; a little of it, at least. Daddy makes me an allowance and I have my own bank account. I'll wire for some money to-day."

Barrett rocked his head on the soft, downy pillows.

"My Lord!" he groaned. "Have I got to go on eating humble pie to the end of the chapter? Wasn't it enough that you should take the risk of marrying a potential convict without having to begin spending your own money on him the first dash out of the box?"

She made a bewitchingly attractive little grimace at him.

"That, you dear old tinderbox, is the very smallest thing we have to consider. Finish your toast and tea and let me lock you in and vanish. Time flies and there are a fearful lot of things to be done between this and dinner."

CHAPTER IX.

THE EMPTY HOUSE.

AFTER Della went away Barrett put in the longest afternoon he had ever experienced. Even with the locked door as a safeguard it didn't seem prudent to take the risk of getting up and dressing. Since the role of sick man had been openly assumed and, so to speak, advertised, it couldn't safely be laid aside.

But no prisoner in shackles and leg irons could have chafed more impatiently. Time and again he buried his head in the pillow and tried to go to sleep, only to emerge, after each attempt, more wide awake than before. Twice during the afternoon some one tapped at his door and tried the knob and each time he listened breathlessly for the rattling of chambermaid's pass key in the lock; but nothing happened.

It was growing dusk when the key rattling did come, finally, and he was ready to leap up and do desperate battle for life and liberty when the lock clicked and the door was opened to admit—not the detective nor the big man with the blond mustache, but the bride of a day, again as a bearer of eatables.

"I simply will not have you making a servant of yourself and lugging trays all over the place for me!" he burst out, exploding in the natural reaction as the fighting stress came off. "Am I to lie here like a sick poodle and do nothing, while you—"

"You are to be a nice boy and do just what you are told to do," was the soothing rejoinder. "By and by you'll have to take the center of the stage, but just now *I'm* playing the star part. Do you feel able to sit up and take a little nourishment? Because, you see, I've brought you a real dinner this time—fried chicken and everything that belongs with it."

"I'm a cross grained bear, Della, dear," he acknowledged, sitting up and making a lap for the well laden tray. "But it is maddening to have you climbing into the breach for me when I am perfectly fit and able to get up and fight my own battles!"

"I am fighting them to a great deal better purpose than you could at the present moment," she returned confidently. "Begin on your dinner while it's hot and I'll tell you the thrilling story of the afternoon while you eat. Lots of things have happened and I've been having adventures."

"I shan't begin until you tell me you forgive me for swearing at you—when I love every hair of your dear head. But I've had such a damnable afternoon!"

"Of course you have! But they also serve who only lie in bed and wait," she paraphrased, adding: "Though that isn't exactly the exciting end of it, I know. I didn't mean to leave you alone for such a long time, but I've been busier than a fly in a spider web."

"Tell me about it," he begged.

"Well, first I hunted up the telegraph office—I didn't dare use the one in the lobby—and wired the Ogden bank for some money. That wasted a lot of time and finally I had to go down to the railroad and get Mr. Hogan's chief clerk to come uptown and identify me. I didn't know banks had to be so awfully fussy and careful. But I got the money at last and we can buy anything we need now."

"It ought to be my money instead of yours," Barrett protested. "I'm still sore about that."

"What's yours is mine, and what's mine is my own," she laughed, misquoting again. "But I hated the time killing part of it; I wanted to be where I could see what the cheddar cheese man was doing with himself. When I came back to the hotel I was relieved to find him sitting in the lobby, smoking a big black cigar and reading a newspaper. I went up to the mezzanine gallery and sat at the railing in a place where I could look down on him.

"For the longest time he never made a move except once to go to the news stand and buy some more cigars. But at last he put the newspaper in his pocket and got up to go out. I fairly flew to get down and chase him before he should get out of sight."

Barrett was fuming over one of the chicken bones. "To think of your having to do a thing like that!" he broke out morosely.

"Dreadful, wasn't it?" she giggled. "The late Miss Della Haynes—now Mrs. James Baxter—daughter of one of Ogden's most prominent citizens, actually shadowing a strange man through the streets of Copah! What wouldn't a bright young newspaper reporter make of that? Never mind; I wouldn't have missed it for anything; it was the most thrilling thing that ever happened to me.

"When I got out of the lobby he was standing at the curb looking up and down the street and for a minute I was afraid he was going to take a taxi and that I'd have to chase him in another. But there wasn't any cab in sight, so he started off walking.

"I followed at a respectable distance—oh, very respectable—but I was careful not to lose sight of him just the same. He went straight out through the town to the hill suburb—Mountain View, they call it—and seemed to know precisely where he was going; you know what I mean—just swung along without looking either to right or left.

"When I was beginning to wonder if he thought there were any mines he could buy out there in that residence suburb, he stopped in front of a handsome place on one of the hill streets; a vacant house with a real estate agency's sign: 'For Sale' on it. He didn't go to the house, which stands back in a little park of its own; he turned in at the driveway gates and went to the garage."

"And there you lost him, of course," Barrett put in.

"Wait. You don't know yet what a resourceful person you have married, Jimsie, dear. The garage is on the lower slope of the grounds and there is a high hedge along that side instead of a fence. Below the hedge there is a vacant lot with a good many of the original pine trees on it. I slipped in among the trees and got as close as I could to the hedge and the garage on the other side of it.

"The hedge is so thick that I couldn't see much, but when I got near enough I could hear two men talking. One of them was the cheddar man—I could recognize his voice. The other had a voice like a saw going through a splintery stick of wood and he swore a good deal."

"Could you hear what they said?"

"Not all of it. But they were wrangling about something—that was plain enough. The swearing man said there wasn't any blankety-blank use of waiting any longer; that if they kept on waiting something would drop. Then they said something—both of them—about 'birds.' The cheddar man asked if there had been any more birds, and the other said: 'Yes, one,' but that the trail 'was still froze.' Then he swore at some third person who wasn't named, and said he wasn't worth the powder it would take to blow him to the hot place."

"And all this, you say, was at the garage of a vacant house?" Barrett queried. "That in itself looks rather suspicious, doesn't it?"

"Lots. But there was more. The swearing man said he'd reached the limit; that he wanted to go and 'take up the claim' without any more loss of time, before somebody else 'got wise and jumped it.' The cheddar man jeered at him and said he had an attack of the 'rattles,' and that made the other man swear some more and say that one of the town bulls had already been around, asking questions about whose car that was in the garage and what its license number was. What did he mean by 'bulls,' Jimmie?"

"Police. They were probably looking for a stolen car. Was there anything more?"

"A little. The cheddar man said they'd wait until ten o'clock to-night; that they could make the drive all right before morning. At ten o'clock, if there were no more birds they would go. But it was pretty plain that he hoped there *would* be some more birds, whatever they are."

Barrett had finished his dinner and he put the tray aside.

"If we are on the right track or any track at all, it is a man's job from this time on," he said firmly. "If you will hand me my clothes—"

"Oh, wait," she protested. "You haven't heard all of it yet. After they had come to some sort of an agreement—about tonight—with the grouchy man still swearing over the additional delay, I heard the garage door slam and the big man came crunching along on the other side of the hedge on his way to the gates. I waited until I was sure he'd be out of sight and then came on back to town as quickly as I could, glad clear down to my toes that I'd had sense enough to wire Ogden for some money."

"So you could hire detectives to keep track of these two?"

"Nothing so silly as that. Didn't you read the newspaper this morning?"

"I did," said Barrett with a recurrence of the shudder that had run up and down his spine at the reading.

"Well, didn't you see that a reward of ten thousand dollars is offered for your apprehension, or the recovery of the money, either or both?"

"I can shut my eyes and see it yet."

"So can I, and it occurred to me that we—you and I—could make much better use of that ten thousand than any detective could. So I went around to one of the motor agencies and bought the most bee-you-tiful car you ever saw; a this year's Stephenson; and told the man to get it all ready and we'd call for it—that we were just married and were going on our wedding tour."

"For Heaven's sake!" Barrett gasped. "What in the world—"

"That is what anybody would say, isn't it?" she inquired sweetly. "But I didn't stop with buying the car; I hunted up a hardware store and bought a pair of the handsomest six-guns you ever laid eyes on—those and an electric torch; and I had the man pack them, with the cartridges, in a pasteboard box and send them to the hotel for me. They're downstairs in the coat room now."

By this time Barrett was reduced to gaping silence as behoved one who had spent his life in measurably well policed cities, taking his adventures vicariously through the columns of the newspapers. But after a moment he found breath to say: If there is to be any shooting I shan't be any good whatever, you know. I've never fired a revolver in my life."

"That is a future," she replied serenely. "If we had time I could teach you; I will teach you some day. But there is some more of the present to talk about. After I had bought the car and the guns I hunted out the real estate people who have the sale of the empty house. They told me the price and all about it—which wasn't interesting, but had to be listened to—and explained that the garage had been rented temporarily to a man from Denver who merely wanted shelter for his car for a few days—possession of both house and garage would be given at any time."

"And then—"

"Then I came back to the hotel. As I was passing through the lobby the clerk stepped out from behind the desk and asked permission to introduce a Mr. Simmons. Honestly, Jimmie, I nearly fainted dead away when I saw that Mr. Simmons was the detective the day clerk had told me about just after luncheon; the man who had found your name on the register and had asked so many questions about you."

"I don't wonder that you felt like fainting," was Barrett's comment. "What did he do to you?"

"He was very gentlemanly and apologetic. He said he had seen my husband's name on the register and had been wondering all day if *my* Mr. Baxter was the Jimmie Baxter he used to know in Chattanooga. Of course, I didn't dare to say that you were not; he could have tangled me up in a minute if I had. So I just played up the best I could; told him yes, that you called Chattanooga home, though you hadn't lived there for some time—I hope that wasn't too barefaced a lie—and added that I was sorry you were too ill to see anybody. He said he was sorry you were sick, but that if you were *his* Jimmie Baxter, he was sure you'd be willing to see him for a few minutes and maybe he could cheer you up and so on.

"I saw he was just bound and determined and that if he couldn't get a chance to see you by fair means, he'd try other ways—and probably succeed. So I said I thought you were asleep, but that if you woke up and felt able later in the evening, I'd let him know."

Barrett sank back among the pillows. "Oh, Lord, that settles it!" he said. "He's probably carrying a photograph of me in his pocket."

"Wait," she said again. "After he had thanked me and said he'd be looking for me this evening I came up one story in the elevator and then went down again by the side stair and out into the street. There is a vaudeville theater in the next block and there, and at a drug store, I found what I wanted."

She was pulling up her sleeves and opening a small package which she had removed from the dinner tray as she entered the room. "Are you going to be a nice, patient boy and let me fix you all comfy and pretty?"

Once more the pure man in Barrett rebelled.

"See here, Della," he stormed, "there's a limit to all things. This dodging business makes me sick at my stomach! I've done a lot of piffling things in my life, but never anything like this. I'm no worm, to crawl into the first hole that offers. Let me get up and meet this Hawkshaw fellow like a man. If worse comes to worse I'll tie him up in a hard knot and throw him out of the window!"

"Much good that would do when he probably has a partner or maybe two or three of them," she put in coolly. "Don't you see how necessary it is for you to keep out of jail when the cheddar man and his accomplice are going to start for somewhere at ten o'clock? Prop yourself with the pillows and let me get to work. And don't forget to be thankful that I served my time with our players' club while I was in college."

With more of the martyr spirit than he had ever thought he could summon, Barrett submitted. It was worth some sacrifice of *amour propre* to feel her fingers in his hair and on his face as she went deftly to work on his disguise and it was only when she fitted a huge pair of shell spectacles on his nose and gummed a neat mustache, clipped in the mode, upon his upper lip, that he let a little groan of anguish escape him.

The transformation wrought, she hurriedly hid the implements of torture in the adjoining bathroom and brought him a hand mirror.

"Take a good look at yourself and see if your own mother would know you," she said, beaming with an artist's pride.

What Barrett saw when he looked in the hand glass shocked him almost as much as if he had found himself staring at his own dead face in a coffin. There was a touch of gray in his hair to make him look at least twenty years his own senior; there were dark hollows under his eyes; the goggling glasses added to the spectral effect; and the mustache, a dead colored lip paste, and the grease paint lights and shadows did the rest.

"Horrible!" he shuddered. "Five minutes more and you would have made a leather faced mummy of me! Nobody would know me. I wouldn't know myself!"

"Well, you are supposed to be a sick man, aren't you?" she inquired airily, manipulating the electric switches so that while there was no appearance of a premeditated attempt to produce a stage effect, the light was tempered somewhat in the region of the bed as if to relieve a sick man's eyes. "Now I'm going to bring Mr. Simmons and you can be conning your lines while I'm gone. You'll carry the part, won't you, dear? Remember—everything depends upon it. I'll be here, but I shan't dare to prompt you with a sharp-eyed detective watching every move."

Normally the least temperamental of persons, as a bank teller should be, Barrett had to fight hard to keep from blowing up when Della left him. Would the disguise fool a man whose daily business it was to penetrate disguises? Would he be able to rise to the occasion and say just the right things to steer the visitor away from the truth and to carry his part so that suspicion would die a natural death and be buried in a grave too deep to permit the possibility of a resurrection?

He doubted it; doubted it fiercely, savagely. The time for preparation was so frightfully short. Any moment Della would be coming back with this man-catcher in tow.

It was now that he cursed the fatuity which had prompted him to register as from Chattanooga, Tennessee. True, he had once spent part of a winter there with his invalid mother, and so knew something of the town and its surroundings. But Della had told the man that he called Chattanooga "home." He must think, *think*. But he couldn't think.

Happily, the torture was not prolonged. At its climax the door was opened and Della appeared, ushering in a smallish man with quick, sharp set eyes and a thin face distorted at the moment by an ingratiating smile. The introduction was informal.

"James, here is a gentleman—Mr. Simmons—who thinks you may be the James Baxter he once knew in Chattanooga. Mr. Simmons, my husband."

Barrett put out a hand with a proper show of hospitality, but the visitor did not take it. Instead, he took one good look at the man in the bed and turned to Della.

"Ah—er—I'm afraid I owe you an apology, Mrs. Baxter—you and your husband both; he is not the man I was looking—er—not my old friend, Jimmie Baxter, of Chattanooga, I mean. The hotel clerk's description quite misled me. Very natural—few people can describe a stranger so that he can be recognized. I can only ask you both to excuse me and—"

Barrett, peering through the goggle-eyed spectacles at his visitor, thought the danger was over. But Della had marked this: that while the man was offering his apology with apparent embarrassment, the sharp-set eyes were taking in every detail of the room, from Barrett's clothes folded neatly upon a chair to the end of one of the telltale black suit cases protruding from behind the footboard of the bed.

"Now that you are here, don't hurry away, Mr. Simmons," she urged hospitably, waving him to a chair. "If you are from Chattanooga, I'm sure my husband will enjoy a visit with you."

Barrett groaned inwardly at what appeared a purely gratuitous prolonging of the agony; but he took his cue promptly.

"Sure! Sit down, Mr. Simmons. It is good to see somebody from the old town, even if I am a case of mistaken identity. Have you been in Chattanooga recently?"

"No, not very lately; not to stop over. But as you say, it is a good old town."

"From this distance in the wild and woolly West it looks a good bit like home to me," Barrett ventured. "This Western mountain country is grand and all that, but I get homesick for old Lookout, don't you?"

"Ah er—yes; very picturesque old mountain—Lookout is."

"And the Inn on top overlooking the city; we've had some distinguished travelers there who have said that the view from the inn porches isn't equaled anywhere else in the nation. You've stopped at the inn?"

"Yes, of course; everybody week-ends up there, sooner or later."

"Recently?" Barrett inquired innocently. "Since they've added the other story and put the observatory on top?"

"Oh, yes," was the ready answer. "I was there last summer for a few days."

Barrett passed his hand over his forehead as if suffering from a sudden twinge of pain.

"Really, I think this upset of mine has gone to my head, Mr. Simmons. Here I go on raving to you about Lookout Inn, and you humor me, when you know, and I know when I'm in my right mind—that the inn was burned down years ago. You'll forgive a sick man, won't you?"

It was the visitor's turn to be embarrassed, and he quickly dragged the talk away from the Tennessee city.

"Don't apologize," he said hastily; and then: "This is your first visit to Copah?"

"The very first. And that reminds me: if you are acquainted here, perhaps you can tell me something about the Little Amy Mining Company?" Barrett drew the company's name haphazard from his memorized list of the Denver bank's out-of-town customers.

"Why—I can't tell you very much about the Little Amy," was the hesitant reply. "The mine is about ten miles from here, I believe—somewhere over in the Juniper range."

"You don't happen to know anything about the financial standing of the company, do you?" Barrett pressed. "They've been buying some machinery of our Chattanooga folks, and—"

"Not a thing," was the hurried reply. There was now less tension of one sort in the air, but more of another and the visitor seemed ready to take his leave. "You—you are out here to collect a bill?"

"Something of that sort," Barrett returned, essaying, and accomplishing, a sick man's smile. His upper lip was itching fiendishly, but he did not dare to put his hand to it for fear of displacing the mustache.

"I'm sorry I can't give you any pointers on the Amy people," said the smallish man. "And I'm sorry you find yourself knocked out. It's the high altitude, I suppose?"

Barrett made a feeble sign of negation.

"The doctors try to tell me that I have a weak heart, but I know better. They can't scare me. I'm all right and I'm going to get up presently and stir around a bit. This lying in bed will do anybody up."

The detective got out of his chair and this time he took the hand that was offered.

"I've gassed with you long enough," he said, returning Barrett's feeble grip with a hearty grasp. "If you'll take a stranger's advice you'll stay right where you are for a while and let the madam nurse you. You may be a sicker man than you think you are."

Then to Della: "I expect to be here for a few days, Mrs. Baxter, and you can even up for this butt-in of mine by calling upon me if there is any little thing that I can do."

She thanked him very sweetly and went to the door with him. "So sorry *my* James Baxter isn't *your* James Baxter," she said, at the moment of leave taking; and stood at the door looking gratefully after him.

CHAPTER X.

DEAD PIGEONS.

WHEN Della reëntered the room Barrett was freeing himself from the clutches of the goggle glasses. "Well, didn't I play up?" he demanded triumphantly. "Didn't I have him squirming to get away? If that is the sort of men the protective associations put on the job I'll say the banks that are paying them don't get much of a run for their money. Why, that fellow is a dub!"

"Don't be too sure about that, Jimmie, dear," she warned. "There is a lot more to Mr. Simmons—whose name, most likely, is not Simmons at all—than appears on the surface. You did hand him a facer when you made him admit that he didn't know very much about Chattanooga and its hotels, and I'm proud of the way you did that.

"But you were not putting anything over on him permanently; I mean so he couldn't turn around and be the suspicious detective again at a moment's notice. I was watching his face—and his eyes—while you talked. I think he came up here fully expecting to find James Barrett; but your disguise—I was shuddering all the time to think how easily we might have overdone that—gave him his second push over in our direction. The newspaper had already given him the first."

"The newspaper?"

"Yes; the evening edition of the *Miner*. When I went down to the lobby just now to tell him he might come up and see you, I had a shock. He had a copy of the *Evening Miner* and was reading the first page stuff. I supposed, of course, it would be something more about you and the robbery, so I slipped over to the news stand before he saw me and bought a paper. We'll have to hand it to Katie Hogan, Jimmie, dear. She's a darling."

"What has she done?"

"She evidently went straight from our wedding to the *Miner* office and tried her best to set us right with the world. There is a front page write up and what Kate couldn't think of, the reporter filled in from his imagination. There is a complete biography of me; and what wasn't known about 'Mr. James Baxter' was just guessed at and put in anyway—old Southern family of Chattanooga—youthful romance while Miss Haynes was in school in the East—and all that."

"Good heavens!"

"Then the write-up went on to say that it had been rumored, quite without foundation as it now appeared, that I was engaged to the absconding bank teller, Barrett; and then it went on to say that while our wedding was extremely private and impromptu this was owing to the fact that the groom was lying ill in the Hotel Intermountain; and there was a lot of silly gush about the touching devotion of the bride in insisting instantly upon a wife's right to take her place at the sick man's bedside."

"Not so much gush about that, either," Barrett put in loyally. "But this newspaper notoriety—it's something terrible for you, Della, dear."

"A lot I care about that! But I do hope the *Miner* doesn't get out to wherever Daddy is. He'll think I have lost my mind. However, perhaps we shan't be here by the time he could hot foot it back to Copah. I have a premonition that we are going to leave town on that wedding tour of ours before very long."

Barrett sat up in bed and hugged his knees.

"I hope you are right. I need action of some sort worse than a lost dog ever needed a bone. But I've been stewing over your discoveries of the afternoon, Della, dear. Really, after all, you know, we haven't anything yet but the wildest of guesses to go on. The only shadow of a starting point is that fat man's order for cheddar cheese and it is perfectly supposable that there are scores of red faced fat men in the world who like an imported cheese with their pie."

"But the talk I overheard?"

"I know; I've been weighing that, too. Didn't you say there is some kind of a mining excitement in the air here?—that that was what took your father into the mountains?"

"Yes."

"Well, the talk you listened to fits into that sort of thing pretty accurately, doesn't it? Didn't the man you couldn't see say something about taking up a claim before somebody else came along and jumped it?"

"Yes; that is what he said."

"There you are, then," said Barrett. "We know that the cheese man claims to be in the mining game and the pair of them probably know of something in this new district that can be grabbed off if they get there at the right moment. There wasn't a word said about money or swag or anything of that sort, was there?"

"N-no," she admitted reluctantly.

"You see how it is," he went on. "We were all keyed up to put our own interpretation upon anything that might happen. We'll have to dig deeper. We would feel pretty cheap if we should go off on a wild-goose chase after a couple of men who are merely mining mad."

"You make me doubtful," she confessed; "but even yet, Jimmie, there is something inside of me that keeps on saying, 'Go to it—go to it!' "

"We will go to it; far enough to find out where these men are starting out for at ten o'clock to-night," Barrett said. "If they strike out in the direction of the new gold field that will settle it definitely."

"And us," she added soberly. "If the cheddar cheese isn't a clew we haven't any clew; that's all."

Barrett was fingering the neatly bobbed mustache.

"Can't I take this blamed thing off now?" he asked. "It makes my lip itch like the very devil."

"Better leave it on until we get past Mr. Simmons in the lobby, don't you think? You may tone down the grease paint a bit to fit the bright lights, but that is about the most that can be done."

"Oh, all right," said Barrett resignedly; "we'll play the monkey-on-a-stick act to a finish. Now, if you'll just hand me my clothes—"

She laid his clothes on the bed and prepared to retreat.

"You are not required to run away," he said. "Aren't we married?"

She paused with her hand on the door knob.

"I'm not so certain of that as I wish I were."

"I'd like to know why you are not. You said 'I do,' and I said 'I do.' And I am sure the minister did his part."

"Yes; but—but you didn't see the license."

"What about the license?"

"Don't you see? I couldn't give your real name; anyhow, not all of it. I'm only Della-Jimmie, or at most, Della-Jimmie-Baxter. Maybe the law will say that I'm only two-thirds married. Maybe we'll have to have it done all over again when you get your surname back."

"Nonsense!" he scoffed, holding out his arms.

"Foolish!" she said with a little laugh; but she stood still and he saw that she was blushing. And before he could speak again she had made some incoherent remark about having to change her own clothes if they were going adventuring, and then she ran away.

The hands of Barrett's watch were pointing to a quarter of nine and he had been up and dressed and pacing the floor impatiently for a full half hour when she came back. At the first glance he scarcely recognized her. She had changed to a smart sport suit of some brownish stuff like khaki, with stout shoes and leggings to match, and her street hat had given place to a soft felt Stetson with a cowboy headstrap.

"How do you like me now and the day you married me?" she bantered. Then, sobering suddenly: "Oh, Jimmie, dear—do we dare go down and out through that lighted lobby?"

"Nothing venture, nothing have," he returned grimly. "If you're ready, let's

go." And he opened the door, fitted his key and flicked off the lights.

Fortunately, they found the corridor empty; and the descending elevator chanced to be empty, also. Not to be too rash, they left the car at the mezzanine landing and paused for a moment at the gallery railing to reconnoiter the lobby floor below. The time seemed to be propitious. A train from somewhere was just in and quite a little mob of travelers was adding itself to the normal evening lobby peopling, stringing in from the street and lining itself up at the registry desk.

"We're lucky!" whispered the young woman; and passing quickly to the broad stair they ran down to lose themselves in the straggling crowd of newcomers. "This way," was the low voiced command, and a moment later Barrett found himself standing at the coat room window with his companion thrusting a heavy paper-wrapped box into his hands.

"The side door!" she directed; and before he could realize how it had been done they were in the street and walking rapidly eastward to circle the block of which the hotel was a part.

They had turned the first corner before he ventured to speak.

"I hope you know where we are going," he said; "I don't."

"I do," she answered. "It is only about half a block farther."

The swift retreat from the hotel ended at the motor salesroom where Della had purchased the Stephenson roadster. The car was ready and they got in, the young woman taking the wheel. Barrett, sitting with the heavy box across his knees, stared at the dash with its unfamiliar furnishings.

"What make did you say this car is?" he asked.

"A Stephenson."

"H-m! You've let yourself in for all the driving. I can drive a gas car, but I don't know the first thing about steam."

"I can drive anything with wheels under it," she boasted; and a few minutes later the silent car was threading the streets of a hilly suburb, and the young woman was steering it around two sides of a parallelogram to come into the street of the empty house in a direction which was leading them back toward the business district.

"You might open that box and take out the things that are in it," she suggested, turning the dash light on and slowing the car to creeping speed as she drew up to park at the curb. "We are almost there."

Barrett opened the box and handled the two formidable weapons gingerly, as befitted a neophyte. Under his window shelf in the bank there had always been a loaded pistol, but apart from looking at it once a day to see that it was loaded he had never paid any attention to it; it was merely a part of the furnishings of the cage.

Rather awkwardly he drew the two weapons from their holsters and loaded them from the cartridge box included in the purchase, trying meanwhile to picture himself confronting two desperate men or possibly three and telling them to put up their hands. The picture seemed grotesquely out of drawing.

"Am I supposed to decorate myself with one of these?" he asked.

"Surely," was the prompt answer. "If these are bad men we're going after they are real bad men—not the movie kind. Buckle the gun on under your coat and let me have the other one."

She had stopped the car at the curb halfway down the grade they had been descending and was setting the hand brake.

"The empty house is just below," she said. "I came in this way so we could get a quick downhill start. We'll leave the car here and walk."

Again Barrett was trying to picture himself as a bold holdup man and this time it was not quite so difficult. The weight of the sagging pistol under his coat was very comforting. The saner half of his brain—the business half— was assuring him that nothing would come of this night stalking of a pair of mining sharks; but the other half, the half that saw a dreary lifetime of flight and exile, not only for himself, but for Della as well—that or its alternate of a long prison term—stretching away before him, was urging him to pin his faith to the hundredth chance that the saner hypothesis would prove to be the wrong one.

Silently, as they passed its grounds, Della indicated the empty house. It stood well back from the street line, and Barrett saw it only dimly in the shadow of the lawn trees. As nearly as he could make out it was a dwelling of the better class, two storied and with a veranda running across the front and around one side.

"Do we break in?" he asked.

"No; I don't imagine we are interested in the house—only in the garage, and that is around on the other side. We'll do as I did this afternoon; get as close as we can under the trees in the vacant lot below."

The approach was made with no special difficulty. Under the low hanging evergreens in the vacant lot they were enabled to creep up quite close to the hedge. There was no light in the garage and no signs of life or occupancy about it. Barrett was beginning to comment upon this when a soft palm was laid quickly over his lips and a whisper at his ear said: "Tobacco, don't you smell it?"

Now that his attention was called to it he did smell it; the acrid odor of a strong pipe. The waiting occupant of the garage was evidently sitting outside in the mild June night, smoking. With one of the two men they were stalking only a few yards away they held themselves silent, almost breathless.

For a time the stillness was broken only at long intervals. Now and again some homing pedestrian passed on the sidewalk, and once there was a rapid fire of exhausts as a car stormed up the hill street with its cutout open. After a time new sounds, low and soothing, like the crooning of a lullaby, began to make themselves heard—*tuck-a-too-too, tuck-a-too-too,* and with them a faint rustling as of perching birds slightly disturbed in the night.

"Pigeons," Barrett breathed. "Where are they?"

"Somewhere about the garage," was the responsive whisper. "I wonder what is disturbing them?"

Barrett's wonder went farther. Pigeons about a city home were a nuisance. Had the former occupant of the suburban house been a pigeon fancier? If so, why had he left the birds behind him when he went away? While these inquiries were passing through his mind there came the crackle and flash of a match.

The smoker on the other side of the hedge was relighting his pipe and the brief flare of the match showed the watchers under the pines the open doors of the garage, with the rear end of a large car visible inside of the small building. On a box with his back against the farther outswung door sat the smoker, a rather muscular, bearded man with a golf cap pulled well over his eyes and wearing the loose, baggy clothes of an amateur sportsman.

After the match went out Della ventured another whisper.

"Did you see them?" she asked.

"See what?"

"The pigeons. They are in that box coop he is sitting on."

This discovery opened up a new vein of questionings. Step by step, Barrett went back over Della's report of the talk she had overheard. Twice there had been some reference to "birds." Were the pigeons the birds?

Slowly the pieces of the puzzle fitted themselves together. The pigeons were carriers and the third man, the one whom this pipe smoker had cursed, was keeping in communication with his associates by means of this ornithological wireless. What were the messages thus transmitted?

Again the business half of Barrett's brain broke in to supply the obvious answer. The third man was on the ground in the field of the new gold strike and the field was out of reach by telegraph or telephone. The man on the ground was to send word when certain conditions were ripe for his confederates in town and upon this information the two others would act.

It all seemed quite simple when it was reasoned out, and Barrett's heart sank. Here was no clew to any robbery unless it might be a robbery in prospect of some unlucky victim in the new gold field.

Barrett was moving cautiously to relieve the strain of his cramped position under the sheltering pine trees when a heavy step sounded on the cement sidewalk a few rods away. Another late pedestrian was climbing the suburban hill street and Barrett felt a cautioning hand laid upon his arm while the lips at his ear framed the words: "That is our cheddar cheese man—I'm almost sure it is!"

The guess was presently confirmed. The footfalls ceased abruptly, there was the click of a gate latch, a creaking of unoiled hinges and then the footsteps began again crunching now upon the loose gravel of the driveway. Through the interstices of the hedge they could see the advancing red dot at the end of a lighted cigar and a moment later the bitter odor of the sitting man's pipe was submerged in a heavier wave of cigar smoke.

"Well," said the newcomer in a voice that seemed vaguely familiar to Barrett, "anything new jumped up?"

"Not a damn thing," was the grunted reply.

"All right," said the other voice evenly, "we'll go. But we're missing the chance of driving the one nail that would make a sure thing of it. I planned this job; neither you nor Canty had the brains to plan it; and you agreed to stick it through.

"Now you've got a case of the twitches and you're hell bent on picking the apple before it's ripe. If you had the brains of a gnat you'd know that the thing would turn out just as I've told you it must turn out—giving it time; and if you had the nerve of a louse you'd be willing to hang on till the clock strikes. Since you haven't either the brains or the nerve—"

The interruption was an explosion of profanity.

"To hell with your high brow work! Five days ago is when we ought to have turned the trick—and look where we'd 'a' been by now! But, no; you had to stick around and sew a fringe onto the edge of it! And make me stick around.

"It's all right for you; *you* ain't got to be feelin' your fat neck all the time to find out if the rope's got there yet! *You* can sit round in the hotel and smoke good cigars and gas with anybody that comes along. But for me and Canty—"

"Cut it out!" was the brittle command. "I've agreed to do what you want to do, haven't I? By doing it we'll be losing the chance that nobody but an impatient fool would lose, but that's a back number now. Get the car out and we'll go. How many birds have you got in that box?"

"Only the three."

"All right; wring their necks and throw 'em over the hedge. And put the box in the car and we'll drop it out somewhere where it won't be found."

A moment later a dead pigeon came flying over the hedge to fall into one of the pines and to drop from branch to branch until it landed within arm's reach of the couple in hiding. Before the second one could be tossed over

Della had given the signal for a hasty retreat.

"We must get back to our car before they start or we'll lose them!" she whispered; and it was at this point that Barrett began to come to his own in the matter of sane foresight.

"We can't go back the way we came in," he objected quickly. "The street light will show us up as we pass. Besides, there isn't time. We must break through and go across lots. Straight ahead; give me your arm!"

The vacant lot was on a rather steep hillside sloping sharply up from the street with a scattering of the small pines all the way up to its rear boundary. At the upper corner they found a thin place in the hedge and forced their way through into what had been the kitchen garden of the vacant house, well in the rear of the garage.

As they came out on the farther side of the hedge a muffled roar told them that the two men had started their motor. This was the signal for more haste. If the car should get away and out of sight they would never be able to trace it.

Together they raced across the weed grown garden, around behind the empty house and diagonally through the grounds in front, dropping over the low retaining wall to the sidewalk. It was a hundred yards farther up the hill street to the place where they had left their car and again they ran, reaching the roadster and climbing into it a mere heartbeat or so before the car they were to follow backed into the street from the driveway below, cut a quarter circle in reverse to straighten itself and shot away townward.

"Don't take your eye off that tail light!" was the young woman's panting plea as she released the brake and opened the throttle of the steam car. "If it turns a corner we'll lose it!"

But the machine ahead turned no corners. Straight on it went until the business district was reached, where it slowed enough to enable the pursuers to come within easy identifying distance. Since the fat man was a guest at the Intermountain, Barrett looked to see the car ahead stop at the hotel, if only long enough to pick up his hand luggage; but no stop was made.

Passing the hotel the flight continued on down the steep street leading to the railroad yards in the valley and crossing the medley of tracks in the yards the leading car turned into the fine State highway running westward through the broad valley of the Pannikin.

When the course was thus plainly indicated Barrett spoke for the first time since the chase had begun.

"Have you any idea in which direction the new gold field lies?" he asked.

Della was throttling the roadster down to keep it from gaining too rapidly upon the car in front.

"It is somewhere in the gulches on Blunt Mountain," she replied. "I don't know just where."

"And Blunt Mountain is—"

"We are headed for it now; or at least in that general direction."

"That settles it," said Barrett gloomily. "We may as well turn around and go back. It is just as I said. Those men are mining sharks on their way to bite somebody in the new field. We've lost."

CHAPTER XI.

THE RED DOT.

QUITE possibly, as a dutiful wife, Della should have stopped the car and given up the chase forthwith; but there was the perfectly legitimate excuse that the highway, which was ditched on both sides, offered no good place in which to turn around.

"We may as well drive on until we come to a cross road where we can back and turn comfortably," she suggested, still with her hand on the throttle.

While they were doing it, with the car ahead advertising its continued flight only by the distance holding red dot of the tail light in the darkness Barrett did some swift thinking. With the one shadowy semblance of a clew lost, what was the use of returning to Copah—to almost certain apprehension and arrest?

Once more the thought of flight laid hold upon him. Suppose they shouldn't go back? Suppose they should keep on to some town on the railroad where the flight—his flight—could be continued by train? With a desperate expedient taking shape in his brain he appealed to Della.

"We're back where we were this morning when I told you in the hotel parlors what had happened to me," he began. "I can't hope to hide in Copah for very long and in the light of the facts so far as they are known I can't blame anybody for believing that I am the thief. Everything points that way and there is nothing to point any other way.

"And we've only made matters infinitely worse by getting married. When the truth comes out—as it's bound to in another day or so at the very farthest—and people find out that you've married the original James Barrett there will be an explosion that will bury you miles deep!"

"Never mind me," was the cool voiced rejoinder. "What about yourself?"

"I am a man and can take my medicine like a man if I have to. But you are not going to be made to take yours—not if I can help it. I love you too well for that."

"Which means that you have a plan?"

"Yes; for what it is worth. The people in the hotel may or may not know that we have gone out together; that makes no particular difference. If you go back alone nobody will remark it."

"But why should I go back alone?"

"I'm coming to that. The only way to stop the explosion is for me to disappear and leave no trace. We are paralleling the tracks of the P. S.-W. You can drive me to a station where I can board a train; and to-morrow morning you can say to the hotel people that I—the James Baxter 'I,' of course—was called away suddenly and took a night train.

"If you'll do that and pay the hotel bill and destroy the contents of the suit cases we left behind and then go home with your father when he comes for you, the whole thing will be buried in a deep grave. Don't you see?"

"I see that you are leaving out the most important thing of all," she retorted quickly.

"And that is—"

"Me," she returned shortly. "Are you assuming that I would consider for one little minute the possibility of letting you go alone? If you have decided to throw up the sponge and run away to South America or somewhere out of reach of the law I shall run away with you, of course. Didn't I promise for better or worse?"

"But see here," he protested vehemently, "that is the very thing I'm trying to stall off—the disgrace for you. If we should disappear together my suit cases would be examined and all my clothes are marked. They'd know then that I am James Barrett and that you had connived at my escape. And would I consent to let you share the lot of a hunted man? Not in ten thousand years!"

"All right," she replied calmly. "Then we go back together and take what is coming to us, whatever that may be."

A branch road opened to the right and she slowed the car preparatory to backing and turning it. As she was reaching for the shift to put the engine in reverse Barrett looked out and saw the red rear light of the touring car ahead suddenly flick to the left and disappear.

"Wait a minute," he interposed quickly. "That car ahead has left the road; either that or its tail light has been turned off."

The young woman left the throttle closed and leaned out to try to determine where they were.

"I visited here with the Hogans last fall, as you know—the time I went deer hunting with them," she said. "I ought to know where we are, but I don't. Isn't that black thing away on ahead a mountain?"

"It is something high enough to cut out a lot of the stars."

"Then it must be Squaw Mountain. If it is, there is a road that leads off to the left somewhere along here. It is a road that goes over the divide and across the Red Desert to Angels and the Timanyoni. Do you suppose they have gone that way?"

"I don't know. The red light just slid over to the left and disappeared."

She was opening the throttle. "We'll investigate a bit," she said. "There is one sure thing about it; that road over the divide doesn't go anywhere near Blunt Mountain and the new gold field—that is certain." And then: "Oh, Jimmie, dear—if we *should* happen to be on the right track, after all!"

Barrett's spirits rose again as the fast car sped along toward the point at which the red light had blinked out. Was the one chance in a hundred going to prove up on itself in spite of all the gross improbabilities?

It still seemed vastly incredible; but when the steam car's headlights showed the turn off to the left and away in the dim distance on the southward bending and ascending side road a tiny red dot appeared, hope sprang up quickened and vigorous. If Della's memory of the topographies was not at fault the two men were *not* going to the new gold field. That much seemed perfectly obvious.

Just as the roadster swung into the left-hand road, Della snapped the lights off. Barrett's protest was fairly jarred out of him.

"You'll never be able to drive without lights!" he gasped as the car surged and bounded over obstructions that could no longer be dodged because they could not be seen.

"It is up to us, isn't it?" she countered. "If we let those men find out that there is a car following theirs that will end it. But you needn't worry. I drove daddy from Ogden to Evanston one night last fall when it was darker than it is now and our lights went bad before we'd gone halfway."

Barrett braced himself and secured good handholds. The red dot was dimming to extinction in the climbing distance, and Della, bending over the big steering wheel and doing her best to keep the car in a road which was little more than a jack trail, was inching the throttle open. For the first few miles the going was a sharp trial, not only to human nerves, but also to the Stephenson, stiff in its newness.

"Here's h-hoping that they g-gave this car all the factory tests and then s-some, before they sent it out," stammered the reckless driver as the powerful car leaped and bounded up an ascent that seemed to be strewn with bowlders and channeled deep with ruts. "If I only knew this road a little bit—but I don't."

Barrett, staring out ahead through the windshield, could see nothing but murky darkness made more opaque now and then by looming mountains, first on one hand and then on the other. At times the red dot ahead disappeared entirely; then a spurt of increased speed would bring it in sight again. Measuring by their own pace, it was apparent that the car they were following was being driven to the full as recklessly as their own, but its driver had the very considerable advantage of being able to run with his headlights on—which made a tremendous difference in his favor.

After possibly a half hour of the blind race in which the grades, although not excessively steep, were all against them, a summit of some kind was reached and a downhill flight was begun. The descent on the southern side of whatever height of land had been crossed was even more perilous than the ascent of the other side had been. It was more abrupt and the road wound in long loops with hazardous turns at each change of direction.

Far below, Barrett could distinguish the red dot racing first to the right and then to the left as the touring car swung down the loop tangents, and now and again he could see the shimmering beam of the powerful head lamps pointing the way for the hard driven machine.

It was not until the last of the perilous grades had whipped to the rear and the Stephenson still trailing the red signal ahead was speeding over what seemed to be a level plain limitless in extent, that Della spoke again.

"Take the flashlight and see how far we have come," she directed; and Barrett found the electric torch and held its beam on the dial of the speedometer.

"It shows a hundred and forty-seven miles; but we haven't covered any such distance as that," he said.

"No; the car had been run a hundred and eleven miles when we took it. I noticed the figures as we drove out of the salesroom."

"Then we have run it thirty-six miles; say thirty-three or thirty-four since we left Copah."

"Thank Heaven for that!" was the fervent rejoinder; and when Barrett asked: "Why?" she explained. "From all I could learn, the new gold field is only some twenty odd miles from Copah, and if we've already come thirty-three—"

"I see," said Barrett. "We're not headed for the gold field; that much is evident. But where are we headed for?"

"Goodness knows. And I haven't the least idea where we are now. If you know anything about the stars, suppose you look out and see which way we are drifting."

Barrett did as he was bidden and after some little craning of his neck found the big dipper and the pole star.

"Just at this moment we are heading a little south of west," he reported;

and as the car took a gentle curve to the left: "Now we are going southwest by south. What are those things on ahead?"

The "things" presently proved to be a double line of telegraph poles standing out stark and ghostly in the treeless waste and a few seconds later the roadster shot over a badly kept-up crossing of a railroad track. Della gave a little gasp of relief.

"That helps out—some," she asserted. "That is the Nevada Short Line track we just crossed, and we are in the Red Desert; I know, because the Short Line and the P. S.-W. are the only railroads running west out of Copah and we know we left the P. S.-W. on the other side of the divide."

"It may help out a lot!" Barrett exclaimed. "The Short Line is the road I hoboed over to get to Copah. We must be somewhere in the neighborhood of the place where I came so near perishing of thirst." Thus far, the linking up process missed the connection between past and present, but the next step bridged the gap.

"Say!" he exploded. "Do you suppose for one moment that those men in the car ahead are chasing back to that cabin in the mountains?"

"Why not? If the cheddar cheese man is the one we've been thinking he was or is. Jimmie, dear, it wasn't a jinx that has been whispering to me all along; it was my good angel. If we lose sight of that car now it will break my heart!"

While the flight and pursuit continued between the wide horizons there was little danger of losing sight of the tiny red eye in advance. Shortly after crossing the railroad track the course swerved to the west again, now and then running near enough to the railway to bring the ghostly procession of telegraph poles into view on the right. For a long time the even pace of the two cars varied little.

As skillfully as if she had been bred to the business of trailing, the young woman at the wheel of the Stephenson held her distance, keeping far enough behind to be well out of sight in the darkness; sight being the only sense to be guarded against, since the silent steam car gliding over the desert sand made no noise to betray its presence.

Once within the first hour of the westward flight a small railroad station was passed with only the light in the telegraph operator's office affording any sign of human occupation. As the red dot in advance made no pause in the hamlet neither did the roadster. After a few more miles had fled to the rear a gibbous moon lifted its misshapen disk above the eastern horizon, casting a weird light over the sage brush plain, and at this Della checked the speed and let the car ahead lengthen its lead somewhat.

"I don't imagine they can see us any better than we can see them," she offered, "but we are taking no chances. Do you recognize anything along this railroad, Jimmie?"

"I wouldn't. I didn't look out after I had climbed into the box car. But I think I would know the side track where I got on. It had a water tank and nothing else but the two switches."

"Is this it we're coming to now?" she asked.

Barrett leaned out to get a better view. The car was passing a blind siding and across the main track appeared the dark bulk of a water tank with water dripping from its staves.

"I couldn't be sure, of course," he qualified, as side track and tank fled to the rear; "it looks enough like it. But if it is it and those men are heading for the cabin, we'll be leaving the railroad very shortly now."

In a few minutes the tentative prediction was verified. Once again the red light on ahead swerved in its course, this time to the left and away from the railroad and at a safe distance the steam car swerved to follow. Step by step the incredible hundredth chance was working itself out to a logical conclusion. Barrett could never have retraced his way unaided to the lonely mountain cabin, but he did know that his general course after leaving it had been to the northeast; and that was the course the two cars were now taking in reverse.

"This is one time when Providence seems to be on the side of the light battalions," he commented. "Those fellows are certainly heading in the way I came out. What do you suppose they are going back for?"

"Don't you see? There can only be one reason," was the quick reply. "The money is there somewhere. Oh, Jimmie—think of it! Perhaps it was hidden right there near you all the time—and you walked away and left it behind!"

At the mention of a hiding place Barrett suddenly remembered the abandoned prospect tunnel in the slope behind the cabin. What safer place could have been found in which to conceal the loot until such time as the robbers might be ready to convey it away? His gorge rose at the cool audacity of the thing. Had they indeed thought so small of him as to leave the money virtually within his reach when he should escape from the cabin?

It was with deep chagrin that he told Della about the old prospect tunnel and how, after actually standing in the portal, he had turned away without so much as a thought of entering it.

"If the money is hidden there we should both be devoutly thankful that you didn't attempt to go in," she replied soberly. "You probably saved your life by not being too curious."

"How so?" he queried.

"Have you forgotten the third man—the one they called 'Canty'? He was probably watching every move you made. And that explains the carrier pigeons. He had them and he was to send them with messages to let the others know when you made your escape from the cabin and what became of you afterward!"

Link by link the chain was growing. Accepting the supposition that the robbers had carried both him and the money to the cabin, it was incredible that they should all have gone away, leaving the immense booty unguarded. And there *was* a third man; that fact was established beyond question: a third man whose duty it was to keep the others informed—about something.

"We are still building upon guesses, but I must confess that right now there seems to be a mighty strong probability that they are going to prove up," Barrett admitted. "In which case it is time we were beginning to plan ahead a bit. What do we do if those fellows in the car ahead pick up the loot and their third man and try for a getaway? As the thing is staged now, they'll beat us to the cabin and we can't help it, since we have to follow them in order to find the way."

The bride of a day had her answer pat. "I'm driving this car, Jimmie, dear, and doing my everlasting prettiest to keep from wrecking it in this no-road. It's up to you to do the ground and lofty plotting."

Now a job in a bank, even that of a teller driven to the limit in the rush hours, does not develop any particular aptitude for wrestling with the physical emergencies. But it may easily do something in the way of sharpening the wits and it puts a high premium upon the ability to make swift decisions.

"I suppose we'll have to be guided somewhat by conditions as they develop," he offered; "but there is one thing certain, Della, girl: if that money is hidden in or around the cabin they are not going to get away with it without a fight."

"Would you, really, Jimmie, dear?"

"Naturally," he returned. "Why else are we chasing them?"

"My-oh! But it does sound good to hear you talk that way!" was the comment this calm assumption elicited. Then: "You may peel that false mustache off now if you want to. I don't believe you are going to need any more disguises. But go on with your plan."

Barrett had quite forgotten the bobbed mustache in the excitement of the chase, but now he removed it and put it away carefully in his pocket.

"It isn't at all likely that there is more than one road to the cabin," he went on, "when I was there I didn't see any road at all. In that case we can't very well get past them to beat them to it, but by the same token they can't get past us to get away. When the time comes we'll block the road with this car of yours and fight it out with them—or rather, I will. You've got to promise me here and now that you'll stay out of it."

She did not make the required promise. Instead: "Would you?" she queried again. "Would you really stand up to three desperate men who probably wouldn't mind killing you any more than anything at all—and you hardly knowing how to pull the trigger of a gun yourself?"

"Well, they can't any more than kill me, can they?" he returned. "And while they're about it I can be trying mighty hard to get some of them. Better let me have that pistol of yours now. Two won't be any too many for me when the trouble begins."

Again she dodged an immediate compliance with his demand. "If daddy could only see you this minute!" she murmured ecstatically. "And he says you're not red-blooded! Jimmie, dear, I'd hug you if I dared take my hands off this wheel!"

Further talk at the moment was interdicted by a happening out ahead. For some reason the car they were pursuing had stopped and it was due only to Della's watchful vigilance that the halt was discovered in time to stop the roadster before it had raced up to certain betrayal of itself. The light was growing stronger as the waning moon crept higher in its arc, but fortunately the scattering sage brush was thick enough to make even as large an object as an automobile indistinguishable at any considerable distance.

"Now whatever do you suppose they're doing?" Della queried, lowering her voice as though she were fearful that she might be overheard in the desert stillness.

"Something gone wrong with their car," Barrett guessed; and the guess seemed to be confirmed when they saw the tiny spark of a flashlight appearing and disappearing in the vicinity of the red dot.

The enforced halt gave them a chance to look about. Directly ahead the dark bulk of a mountain range outlined itself in the wan moonlight and it became apparent that the two speeding cars had covered in the time measurable by less than an hour a distance which it had taken Barrett a long day's tramping to traverse.

That the mountains in the foreground were those in which the abandoned cabin stood, Barrett had little doubt. And that there must be a practicable road up to the bench upon which the cabin was built was sufficiently indicated by the fact that he must have been transported thither in a vehicle of some sort; most likely in the same auto which was now halting for repairs a short quarter of a mile away.

"Aren't you getting mighty tired of hanging on to that wheel?" he asked of his companion in the driving seat.

"No; I'm good for still more of it. I've driven daddy a lot in the past year."

"It's a shame that my steam car education has been neglected," he said, "but I don't know the first thing about them. How do you regulate the fire and the water in the boiler?"

"I don't. They regulate themselves automatically. The only thing I'm worrying about is the tank supply of water. We're pretty nearly out and if we don't come to a creek when we reach the mountain, we'll be in trouble."

"Why did you choose a steam car?" he asked.

"Because I've driven them a lot and I know what they will do. That is a big Stanhard ahead of us, and you know how a Stanhard will run when you step on it. But this car could give it a mile start and catch it in the next mile. I wanted to be able to do just that if we had to."

"Wise little head," he praised. And then: "Della, dear, I'm like the man who found a precious jewel in the middle of the big road and didn't realize what it was until a miracle came along and opened his eyes. But for the horrible mess the bank's money has made for us I might never have known what a magnificently loyal little running mate I was getting."

"Oh, thank you!" she said with a strained little laugh that had just a hint of physical weariness in it. And after a moment: "I don't imagine either of us will ever forget this wedding day of ours, Jimsie, dear; do you?"

"I hope I shall be properly punished if I do."

"It's precious in a way, too," she went on musingly. "We don't know yet how it is going to end; but we've lived a whole beautiful lifetime since this morning, and—oh, my dear! I'll never be afraid of you any more!"

"Afraid of me?" he exclaimed. "What ever put that into your mind?"

"You'll laugh and say it's silly; and perhaps it is; it was just a woman's fear of the—of the thing that can never be undone; it's deep in every girl's heart, I think, no matter how sophisticated she may be or how much she has mixed and mingled with men socially.

"We are all cave people yet, Jimmie, under the skin, and to-day, when I promised to 'love, honor, and obey,' I had a real cavewoman's little shudder at the thought of what some men, and perhaps you, might make that mean to me. But it's all over now."

"I should hope so!" he said, taking her in his arms and for a moment the hazardous chase, the weird surroundings and all thought of what the next hour might bring forth were blotted out.

It was the young woman who first broke the ecstatic spell. "Listen!" she said, freeing herself quickly. "Isn't that the noise of their motor?"

It was. The car ahead was once more in motion and the red dot was growing visibly smaller. Skillfully Della worked the Stephenson up to speed. Adding his vigilance to hers Barrett kept his eyes fixed upon the tiny signal which was now threatening to disappear entirely.

"A little more throttle if you dare," he urged. "They are outpacing us."

The increased speed was promptly forthcoming, but at the moment when the gap seemed to be closing a little the red light blinked out suddenly.

"What does that mean?" Barrett demanded.

"We'll find out in a minute," was the determined reply; and as it was given the fast roadster with full power on crashed through and over the sage in a magnificent burst of speed toward the point at which the red signal light had disappeared.

CHAPTER XII.

RED BLOOD.

THE cause for the disappearance of the red light became apparent as soon as the racing roadster reached the place where they had had their final glimpse of the small signal. The road, fairly distinguishable, now that the moonlight was picking it out, had entered upon a winding course among the foothills of the mountain range and its crookings, limiting the view ahead, added a new peril to the pursuit.

"Here is where we take our lives in our hands, Jimmie, dear," Della remarked as she swung the heavy car to right and left around the short curvings of the road. "They have had to stop once for repairs, and if they do it again, we'll be into them before we know it."

Her unperturbed courage was contagious. Barrett drew his weapon from its holster and was surprised to find that his nerves were quite steady; now that the crisis was approaching his only anxiety was for the safety of his companion. If the men in the car ahead were the desperate characters there was now every reason to believe they were, they would probably open fire at once if they should be overtaken.

"Listen," he urged; "I want you to do exactly as I tell you. If we should find them stopped again and run up on them unexpectedly, you slide down out of sight where the machinery under the hood will protect you from their bullets. Will you do that?"

"I hear what you say," was the noncommittal answer.

"But will you do as I say?"

"I'll take care of myself—yes."

"One more question," he thrust in hurriedly. "I don't know very much about weapons: do I have to cock this thing first or will it fire if I just pull the trigger?"

"Just pull," she instructed, without taking her eyes for an instant off the winding road. "It's a double action. And hold it low—under what you're shooting at. Until you have learned the balance of a gun it will always jump a little and shoot high."

He marveled at the coolness with which she gave these directions while she was whisking the storming car at breakneck speed around the twistings and turnings in the hilly road. And although they had not yet regained enough of the touring car's lead to bring it in sight again it was with a sigh of relief that he found Della checking the headlong pace at the bottom of one of the hills where the road crossed a trickling stream.

"Water," she said, stopping the car with its front wheels in the stream. "I don't dare to try another hill climb without filling the tank. When we get into the mountains it will be all uphill."

Barrett sprang out, got the canvas bucket out of the deck locker and, working rapidly under her directions, replenished the water supply. The enforced stop was not long, but minutes even on the poor road might easily mean half miles in increasing the lead of the car ahead and thus further complicate matters.

"Half a tank—that's enough," she announced; and as Barrett climbed to his place she opened the throttle again and the race was resumed.

A short half mile beyond the ravine of the creek the road left the foothills and began to climb the backgrounding mountains, looping the gulch heads in thick timber and doubling the points of the shouldering spurs.

Barrett wondered why a fairly practicable road should have been made in such an isolated wilderness, but the query answered itself shortly when they began to pass, along the foot of the upper slopes, wide stretches from which the timber had been cut. Evidently, the road had once been an outlet for a lumbering company.

Della, bent over the wheel in a ceaseless effort to steer fine enough to keep from plunging the car over the precipices that threatened all the way along, spoke only once in the storming climb and that was to ask Barrett how far he thought it might be to the cabin.

"I can't tell," he answered. "I can only guess from the height we've reached. It can't be much farther now."

As he spoke, the climax they had been more than half expecting leaped out at them. As the roadster rounded a sharp curve they both saw the red light signal less than a hundred yards ahead and it was standing still. Luckily, the curve was on a stiff upgrade, so the roadster was brought to a stop within its length. With admirable presence of mind, Della put the engine in reverse and let the car roll silently backward down the grade and out of sight around the curve and at a safe distance she stopped and set the brakes.

"Did they see us?" was her first whispered query.

Barrett had pocketed the electric torch and was softly unlatching the door on his side. "I think not," he answered. "They would have fired at us if they had."

"What are you going to do?"

"This is our chance—or rather mine. We can't be far from the cabin, and they are evidently stalled again—something wrong with their car. I'll cut around and get in ahead of them. There is the one chance in a million that the money may be cached in the old tunnel and if I can get to it first and find it and get away with it while they are stopping here tinkering their car, it will be that much to the good. While I'm gone, you back down until you can find a safe place to turn around and then you'll be ready to make a run for it when the time comes."

"And let you go and get killed all by yourself?" she replied indignantly. "I think I see myself doing anything like that! I'm going with you."

It was quite in vain that he argued, pleaded, begged while the precious moments wasted themselves.

"I'd much rather die with you than live without you, Jimsie, dear," was all the answer he could get; and in the end he yielded as the bridegroom of a day must. "All right," he consented at length; "if you must, you must. But I'll never forgive myself if anything happens to you. Come on; what we do must be done quickly."

Fortunately for the detouring experiment the stop had been made at a spot where the timber grew thickly and leaving the car as it stood they turned aside from the road on the up-mountain slope and climbed among the trees to a safe height before venturing to press forward. Having taken this precaution, they were well up on the forested slope when they passed the stalled touring car.

As they looked down upon it the moonlight enabled them to see that the hood was lifted and that both of the occupants were out and doing something to the machinery. Cautiously they crept on, holding a course parallel to the road and still well above it. After going only a short distance beyond the stalled car they saw a dark figure coming down the road at a brisk walk.

"The third man!" Della whispered; and they stopped and stood motionless among the trees until the figure disappeared around a bend in the road.

"That clears the field for us!" said Barrett jubilantly. "A little time is all we need now—but we're not likely to have any too much of that. They'll get that car going again in a few minutes, and then it will be all over but the shouting—or the shooting. I wish to the Lord you had stayed with the roadster. That one little thing is all I lack of being happy."

"Yes; and a nice time I'd be having, wouldn't I?" she retorted. "It's no use; you can't shake me off, Jimmie, dear. I'm a part of you now and I'll be with you at the finish, whatever it may be."

They reached the little plateau upon which the deserted cabin stood sooner than they expected to. It was such a perilously short distance up the road from where the two men—or probably the three, by this time—were still tinkering at the stopped car.

Barrett led the way around to the front of the log shack. The door was standing open, and a handful of fire was burning upon the hearth. Obviously the third man had been camping in the cabin.

Beside the door there was a cracker box transformed into a bird cage with slats nailed across its open side. Barrett snapped the switch of the flashlight and a pair of pigeons stirred uneasily in the corner of the box coop and crooned their *tuck-a-too-too*. "That is the other end of their wireless," he said. Then, turning the light into the cabin: "I don't suppose there is any use in our wasting time here. If they've hidden the money it will be in a safer place than this."

"The mine tunnel?" the young woman suggested.

"Most probably. We'll see."

It was only a short distance to the dark hole in the slope behind the cabin. As they stood together under the rotting timber portal, Barrett recalled the brief glimpse he had had of the place in the flare of a single match before dawn on the morning of his escape. Under the beam of the electric flash lamp nothing new was revealed. A few feet beyond the entrance the roof had fallen in, and a mass of broken rock and earth quite filled the tunnel, although the gaping chasm overhead, out of which the cave-in had fallen, appeared to offer a passageway to the depths beyond where they stood.

"Will you hide out among the trees and wait for me while I climb and see what I can find?" Barrett asked, pleading again.

"Not I!" was the shuddering reply. "Don't you see what that would m-make me do? If they should come up while you were in there, I'd simply have to shoot them d-down, one at a time, to keep them from getting at you! You wouldn't make me do such a dreadful thing as that, would you? I'd be-be obliged to, you know."

"You brave little soldier!" he exclaimed in husbandly exultation. "I believe you would do that very thing! Come on; we'll go in together." And together they scrambled over the heap of earth and rock, finding beyond it a measurably unobstructed passage leading on to an unknown distance in the heart of the mountain.

As it chanced, they were not constrained to explore the gloomy cavern to its farthest depths. Less than fifty yards beyond the obstructing roof fall, Barrett, who was sweeping the jagged walls on either hand with the beam of the flash light as they went along, turned the light of the torch into a narrow niche on the right. At the back of the niche, which was nothing more than a crevice, shot out in a softer stratum of the rock by one of the tunnel blasts, stood a black painted powder canister partly covered by a gunny sack.

Barrett gave the torch to his companion and fished the canister out of its hiding place. By its weight he could tell that it was filled—with something; not powder, because it wasn't heavy enough for that.

His hands were shaking as if he had been suddenly stricken with an ague when he put the black can down on the tunnel floor. The top had been cleanly cut around the edge, though not quite all of the way around, and it was wired in place. The wire was stiff, but he knelt and twisted at it with bare fingers until it came off. When the cut cover was lifted, one glance at the contents of the can was enough. The powder container was stuffed full of packages of bank notes.

"Oh! Thank Heaven!" gasped the pretty torch holder, and the exclamation was more than half a sob.

"It's here—some of it, at any rate," said Barrett, bank trained coolness taking possession of him at sight of the money. "Will you hold the light down while I count it?"

"C-count it!" she said, with a little shriek. "Why, it will take *hours* to count it—and those men may be here any minute!"

"Oh, no; it won't take seconds," Barrett returned, dumping the packages of bills on the floor and handling them swiftly. Thirty nine of the forty parcels were intact, with the printed "$5,000" binding slip of the bank on each. But the fortieth had been broken and rewrapped with a string; and this one was five hundred dollars short.

"This is the one they broke to give me five hundred dollars that I couldn't spend," he said, and was beginning to cram the money back into the can when Della protested shrilly.

"You can't carry that thing!" she pointed out. "Put it in the gunny sack, and for pity's sake, *hurry!*"

The little tremolo of panic in her voice made Barrett stop and look up at her in amazement. Hitherto she had been all cold courage, and he had been the one to need bolstering. But now they seemed to be changing places.

She was trembling with impatience to be gone, while he found himself growing stubbornly unwilling to hurry; more than unwilling—not wishing to go at all until he had staged a final climaxing act with the men who had not only robbed him, but had concocted a devilish plot to steal his good name and send him to rot in prison. Was he to be satisfied with a simple recovery of the loot and let these scoundrels go free? Hardly.

"All right," he said in reply to her plea for haste, "we'll get out in the open if you'd rather; though if there were any place in here where I could hide you out of bullet range, I'd just as soon settle with those beggars here as anywhere." And he began to chuck the packages of money into the sack.

"What do you mean, 'settle'?" she chittered. "Haven't we got what we came for—if we can only be l-lucky enough to get away with it."

"I mean just what I say," he returned doggedly. "The game isn't played out yet, and it won't be until after I've had my innings."

"Bu-but this isn't red blood, Jimmie, dear!" she wailed; "it's just c-crazy sus-suicide!"

"That, dear girl, is what I'm going to try to make these fellows think it is before I'm through with them. Let's go. Stick closely behind me and snap that light off as soon as you can find your way without it."

Against all the probabilities, they escaped from the tunnel without being intercepted, although the margin of safety was measurable in seconds. They could hear voices on the other side of the cabin, and they had barely time to draw aside in the shadow of the trees when the three men came around the corner of the shack.

The fat man was in the lead, lighting the way with an electric torch, and the smallest of the three, the one they had seen going down the road toward the stalled automobile, was explaining volubly.

"How t' hell was I goin' to know 'at I couldn't trail the geezer?" he snarled. "You said I wasn't to let him know anybody was keepin' cases on him. I've tramped more 'n a hundred miles since he broke loose, tryin' to find out where he'd gone to!"

"Shut up!" snapped the big man in advance. "You've balled it—that's all. You can talk 'til hell freezes over, but that's what it comes to."

Quite methodically Barrett drew his revolver from its holster and aimed it at the leading man. It was only his ineptness with the weapon that gave the bride of a day time to throw herself upon him before he could pull the trigger; and by the time the silent little struggle was ended, the three men had disappeared in the tunnel.

"Oh, good Heavens, Jimmie, dear!" she panted, "have you lost your mind? Let's run! We can reach our car before they overtake us! Come, quick, before they come back and find out what's been done to them!"

"You may go," he gritted. I want you to go—and take this sack of stuff along with you. But when I go, these bandits go with me—dead or alive."

"Oh, you glorious fool!" she wept, throwing her arms around his neck.

"Are you going to make a widow of me before we've been married a day? You can't fight three of them. They'll kill you, and then what will become of me?"

A faint glow of the returning flashlight was beginning to show in the depths of the tunnel, and Barrett freed himself masterfully and thrust the sack of money upon her.

"Take it and fly," he commanded brusquely. "Run on down to the car and I'll be with you when the show is over. I'm not going back to Copah empty-handed. *Run*, I tell you—while you have a chance! The bullets will be flying here in a second or two, and whatever happens, that money's got to be saved!"

"Oh, don't send me away!" she begged. "If you've got to stay, let me stay and f-fight with you!"

"Never in this world. This is a man's job. If you love me, take that sack and run with it!"

Thus adjured, she snatched up the sack and ran—a little way. As she reached the corner of the log cabin she saw the big touring car standing before the door. It had been turned around and was headed for the flight down the mountain. Her first impulse was to drop the sack of money and try to disable the car, thus making pursuit with it impossible if Barrett should come to his senses and run while there was yet time for flight.

But time was no more. Even as the thought flashed into her mind, the three men came stumbling out of the tunnel; two of them accusing the third and cursing him savagely.

"You damned coyote"—it was the harsh voice of the touring car driver that was ripping sawlike into the high mountain silence—"d'you think f'r a holy minute you can double cross us like this and get away with it? Drop that gat 'r I'll bore you right where you stand! Now you've got 'til I can count ten to tell us what you've done with the swag! One—two—three—"

The interruption was a sharp command of "Hands up!" from the tree shadows, and the counting stopped abruptly. According to the time honored custom firmly established by the scenario writers and armchair annalists of wild Western moments of stress, the three men should have reached for the stars in prompt capitulation.

But they did nothing of the sort. Instead, two of them opened fire instantly upon the tree shadows, while the third stooped to grope for the gun he had just dropped at the threatening command of his accuser.

It was all over in a minute. The banging fusillade was answered by spiteful spurts of fire from the tree covert; one of the three—the one who had stooped and was rising to get into action—staggered and sank back to his knees; and the next instant the other two had darted back to cover in the tunnel, dragging the wounded man with them.

After that, silence, profound and unbroken even by the whispering of the night wind in the pines, descended like a thick cloud upon the scene of the late crackling of firearms.

CHAPTER XIII.

GREASE PAINT.

FOR the young woman crouching at the corner of the log cabin the blank silence was horrifying. Quite naturally, her first thought was that Barrett had been killed, and for an instant the cabin and its surroundings swam in dizzy circles for her. But the lapse of self-control was only momentary.

Dropping the sack of bank notes she flew across the little clearing to the shelter of the trees, calling softly: "Jimmie! Oh, Jimmie, dear, where are you?"

Barrett was not dead. When she found him he was sitting on the ground behind one of the larger trees, trying to bandage a flesh wound in his left arm with strips torn from a shirt sleeve.

"Oh, my dear!" she gasped, kneeling beside him. "Have they killed you?"

"Not yet," he returned grimly. "It's only a scratch, but I thought I'd better tie it up. The blood makes everything so messy and sticky."

It was she who did the bandaging, deft fingers flying swiftly.

"It was so perfectly reckless!" she murmured. "Didn't you *know* they'd begin to shoot as soon as you called to them?"

"I supposed they would—yes. But I had cover of a sort and they were in the open. And because they hadn't sense enough to duck I got one of them. Did you see him drop? I'll get the others before I'm through with them. What have you done with the money? And why didn't you go on down to the car as I asked you to?"

"And leave you here to be killed? I couldn't go. You knew I wouldn't go without you."

"But the money," Barrett insisted.

"Oh, it's over there by the cabin. It won't run away until we run with it. And that is what we are going to do, as soon as I get this arm tied up."

"Not me," Barrett denied, resolutely disregardful of his English in his new character. " 'Dead or alive,' I said. I'm going to get all three of these sham bad men before I quit. If they get out of that tunnel alive they'll come with their hands up. Is that their car out in front of the cabin?"

"It is. I was just wondering if I couldn't disable it some way when the shooting began."

"We mustn't cripple that car. By the time I'm through with these buccaneers we're going to need it—either for an ambulance or a hearse."

"For mercy's sake!" she breathed. "And daddy said—"

"I know what your father has said," Barrett broke in. "I suppose I might have gone along indefinitely, giving all the scraps and street rows a wide berth and cosseting myself like a sick lamb. But that's a back number now. I'm getting my teeth into the real thing, and by George, it tastes good to me!"

"But, Jimmie, dear!" she pleaded. "You can't get them out of that tunnel unless they come of their own accord! And when they find out there is only one of you—"

"They are going to find out at that same moment that the one is a whaling plenty," he boasted belligerently. "Hand me that coat and let me get some more cartridges out of the pocket."

"*Jimmie!* Do you want to break my heart? You're not going into that black hole to get killed!"

"Sure I'm not. It's the other fellows who are going to get killed if they won't listen to reason. I've told you what's due to happen. They're going to Copah with us—dead or alive. It's up to them to decide which way they prefer to go. I'm not particular."

"Oh, you glorious, *glorious* fool!" she exclaimed rapturously. "I—I'd give worlds if daddy could see you now!"

"I'm not exactly on exhibition," he snorted; "but neither am I any longer a monkey on a stick. Hold my coat for me and stay right here behind this tree. I'm going in after those make believe brigands."

It was all to no purpose that she begged and pleaded again, trying to show him that he had done all that any one man could be expected to do; that they could disable the robbers' car and reach their own in safety with the money if they should go at once.

"It's no manner of use, Della, dear," he said when she stopped for lack of breath. "I wouldn't back down now if the whole financial system of the universe depended upon it. It's all or nothing: I want those beggars in that hole and I'm going to get 'em."

Of course, she had to let him go. She wasn't quite the kind of young thing to wrap her arms around him and try to hold him. Hovering behind the sheltering tree bole, she saw him slip out and dart across the moonlit space.

At the tunnel mouth he disappeared, and there was an agonizing interval before anything else happened. But by the time anxiety and the prolonged suspense were threatening to drive her mad a curious monster that seemed to be chiefly legs and arms attached to a single body came tumbling out of the tunnel's mouth to roil and wallow in strange and grotesque contortions all over the small open spaces between the hill slope and the cabin, emitting savage curses in two separate and distinct voices, the maledictions mingling with thudding blows, as it leaped and floundered.

It was the Barrett half of the monster that disentangled itself and rose up after the wallowings were quieted, and he was brandishing the revolver with which he had clubbed his big bodied antagonist.

"One!" he shouted triumphantly at the tree shadows and promptly dived back into the tunnel.

This time the bride of a day heard muffled shots, three or four of them, and stopped her ears in wifely terror. But after another interval which seemed doubly age long, a single figure appeared at the tunnel portal. It was leaning far forward, trudging manfully and dragging two other figures, both limp and unresisting.

"I told you I'd get 'em!" Barrett panted as she ran out. "They may not all live to get to Copah—I'm not so sure about that part of it—but they're going there just the same!"

"But you?" she faltered. "You're all bloody! Where are you hurt?"

"It's nothing; I got a crack over the head in that last tussle, that's all. But you'll notice that I've made the riffle. I said I would and I did. Run and get the blankets out of the cabin and we'll truss these birds up."

"I—I don't think I knew you at all before to-night, Jimmie, dear," she stammered; and then she fled to do his bidding.

As it transpired in the trussing process, Barrett had made a thorough job of it with his clubbed revolver, and there were only relaxed and sodden bodies to work upon as he bound his captives with their own belts, the tow rope and even the tire chains, after having made a rude first aid dressing for the small man who had been shot in the leg in the first exchange.

"I hope I haven't killed any of 'em," he said when the trussing was completed, adding vindictively: "I want to see 'em sent where they were meaning to send me, by Jove!" Then, in victorious gloating: "Wasn't it a lovely scrap? But I'm forgetting—you didn't see much of it."

"I s-saw you when you stood up and shouted 'One'!"

"That was the cheddar cheese hog. He was just inside of the tunnel, trying to peek out, and I stumbled over him first. Got his gun and a grip on his gullet before he could shoot or yell for help. He didn't last long—too fat."

"And these others?"

"They were easy. They were over behind the fallen roof and this little one was already crippled. The black whiskered bird emptied his gun at me, but he was rattled and couldn't shoot straight. Guess he thought I was ten or a dozen instead of just one man. He clubbed me once before I laid him out. Can you back that car of theirs around here where it will be handy?"

"I'm as nervous as a s-scared cat, but I'll try," she assented, and went to do it.

With the big touring car backed into position, the next problem was how to get the three unconscious captives into it. Barrett solved the problem by tearing the cabin bunk bedstead to pieces and laying the planks as an inclined plane up which they slid and rolled the human lading. The fat man gave them the most trouble, but by dint of a lot of pulling and pushing and prying with the planks, they got the inert mass of him up into the tonneau, after a time.

"There!" said Barrett, slamming the tonneau door upon the disorderly heap of humanity tumbled in without regard to riding ease or even tolerable comfort. "Now let's see if you'll poison anybody else's coffee!" Then to the bride of a day: "Look me in the eye, Della, girl: Am I, or am I not, red blooded enough to come up to your father's idea of the kind of man he wants for a son-in-law?"

"You—you've got me all fuddled up and dazed, Jimmie, dear," she stammered. "You—you're so different! What did it?"

He laughed. "It's the reaction from the monkey-on-a-stick part you made me play in the hotel. Did you think you were marrying something less than a man? Let's go. It's a long way back to Copah."

With the money sack salvaged, Barrett kicked the slats off the pigeon coop so that the birds could escape, and then, climbing to the driving seat of the touring car he took the wheel and the descent of the mountain was begun. When they came to the curve in the road, where the roadster had been left, he stopped the car and got out.

"You've had excitement and hard work enough for one night," he told Della, "and I'm not going to let you drive that car to town. I'll slack the brake and let it run back into the ditch, and we'll send somebody out here after it to-morrow. Keep your gun handy and pull it down on those fellows in the tonneau if they wake up while I'm gone. This boat is an ambulance, now, but we won't mind turning it into an undertaker's wagon if they insist upon it."

Suiting the action to the word, he climbed into the roadster and let it run backward until there was room to pass. Once more in his place behind the wheel of the touring car, he issued his final order.

"Now you cuddle down and go to sleep, if you can. I can find the way back to town with this truck load of stunned hogs, and there isn't a thing you can do if you try to stay awake. This isn't just my idea of a wedding tour—hasn't been, from the first—but we'll make it serve. Kiss me just once, dear, in honor of the occasion, and—"

When she sat up, he saw by the light of the dash lamp that she was wiping her lips.

"What was it—blood?" he asked, as he let the big car go racing down the grades.

"No; grease paint," she said; and with that she snuggled down beside him and closed her eyes.

CHAPTER XIV.

CHEDDAR CHEESE.

IN the graying dawn of a flawless June morning, early risers in the thriving little mining city of Copah saw a seven-passenger automobile, red from radiator to rear tank with the dust of the desert, limping on an inadequate number of cylinders up the hill street leading from the railway yards.

In the driving seat sat a young man, hatless and hollow eyed, with a caking of the red dust in his matted hair, and beside him was a young woman asleep, with her head on the chauffeur's shoulder, her face and natty suit of sport clothes also covered with the red dust, and her cowboy hat rakishly cocked over one eye.

In the roomy tonneau was a lading at which the early morning onlookers stared in astonishment. Crouched on the floor of the car, with the rear seat for a back rest, were three men in various stages of dishevelment; a fat man with a blond mustache; a dark faced man, bearded, blood stained and angry eyed; and a third, smaller than either of the others, whose face was a harsh mask of pain.

It was at the main entrance of the Hotel Intermountain that the dusty automobile drew up. Very gently the haggard chauffeur awakened his seatmate, while a little knot of early pedestrians gathered to stare at the singular spectacle afforded by the travel worn car and its strange occupants. Through the revolving doors of the hotel came a detachment of bellboys intent upon tips; and at sight of the gathering crowd a policeman sauntered up.

"What the divvle will it be?" queried a railroad yardman on his way to work, asking of the nearest ear.

"Movie outfit, I guess; been out in the desert shootin' a film for a hold-up," was the answer. "Yuh can seen the grease paint on that feller's face, and the stuff that's made to look like blood—never stopped to wash it off. And look at the skirt: ain't she a peach—dirt and all?"

The hatless driver of the dusty car was clambering out stiffly, dragging a half-filled gunny sack after him. A nearer view showed that his "make-up" was faultless; almost corpse like.

One of the bystanders whispered to another: "By George, if that isn't blood on his face and in his hair, I'll eat my hat! Why, look; you can see the cut and the swelling! Them movie stunters don't stop at nothing, do they?"

By this time the chauffeur was helping the young woman out of the car, and it was noticed that he stood with one foot on the half-filled gunny sack while he did it. As the sauntering policeman, accepting the moving picture explanation of the scene as the true one, was moving away, the young man who had failed to remove his "makeup" beckoned to him.

"Officer, can you drive a car?" he asked quite casually.

"And if I can—what then?" demanded the majesty of the law.

"I was going to say that you might drive this car around to headquarters and have these three birds in the tonneau locked up for safekeeping."

"Say; ain't you movie actors?"

The young man shook his head. "Only in the sense that we've been on the move the better part of the night—out across the Red Desert and back."

Shouldering his way through the throng that was now blocking the sidewalk, the big policeman looked in upon the tonneau lading. "Hell's bells!" he said; "so *that's* why they ain't sittin' on th' seat! Who done th' job o' hog-tyin'?"

"I did," replied the chief actor modestly; then apologizing for the manner: "It's not a very workmanlike job, I'll admit. I had nothing but substitutes for handcuffs and shackles, and I had to make up in quantity what the stuff lacked in quality. If you'll take these men to headquarters and have them doctored up and jailed, I'll appear a little later and make the charge against them."

While he was speaking, the smallish man whose name on the hotel register was Simmons, had wriggled up to lay a hand on the chief actor's shoulder.

"Oh, no; you don't make any such grand stand play as that, Mr. James Baxter Barrett," he said quietly. "I'm on to you with both feet, this time. You are arrested for the theft of two hundred thousand dollars from your own bank. And we're going to make your wife—if she is your wife—an accessory after the fact. You may as well come clean. What have you done with that money?"

Before the accused one could reply, an elderly man, grizzled, gray, and with a granite like face and the underslung jaw of a ring fighter, had come through the revolving doors to push his way to the curb. At sight of him, the young woman, poised on the running board of the automobile, leaped into his arms with a cry of "Daddy!"

Barrett was grinning into the face of the smallish man, and if the grin could have been caught on a motion picture film it would have made his fortune.

"You are just a few hours too late, Mr. Simmons," he countered. "If you had arrested me last night when you came to my room and let me tangle you up on the geography of Chattanooga, you would have stood a good chance of fingering the big reward. I hadn't any alibi then, but I have one now."

"Where is it?" was the snappy demand.

"Right here," Barrett returned, picking up the dusty gunny sack. "One hundred and ninety-nine thousand five hundred of them, in fact. You see, Mrs. Barrett and I had the clew—the real clew—and we were obliged to pull off the little theatrical stunt on you to keep you from jailing me before we could get action.

"Now, good people," he went on, pleading with the sidewalk jam, "if you'll be good enough to let us through—there are two of us needing a hot bath and breakfast worse than a stray pup ever needed a bone."

A COUPLE of hours later, at a table for three in the Intermountain dining room, Barrett, bathed, shaved, clothed, and in his right mind, was sitting opposite a bright faced young woman whose dark eyes were dancing. Between them, at the table end, sat the grizzled elderly man with the underslung jaw, methodically putting away his breakfast as he listened to his daughter's story of the adventures of the night.

"What did you think when you came back and found that I was married, Daddykins?" the young woman asked, after the adventures had been duly spread forth.

"Huh!" growled the mine owner father, "you didn't fool me for a single minute. Hogan met me at the train and told me you'd married a stranger from Tennessee; and I told him he lied. You see, I knew it was Jimmie you'd married, and not anybody else under the shining heavens."

"Of course you did. But did you really believe that Jimmie had stolen two hundred thousand dollars from his own bank?"

The elderly man looked up from beneath his shaggy eyebrows at the two younglings, first at one and then at the other.

"I'll leave it to you both!" he exclaimed, "if it didn't look that way. How was anybody going to believe anything else?"

"You were entirely justified," said Barrett equably. "It was up to me to prove that I didn't. But I should never have been able to do it if Della hadn't jumped in and helped. It was her good work and wit that kept me going. At the very last, when we were chasing those fellows out of town, I wanted to turn back. I thought we were on the wrong trail. But Della wouldn't have it that way; and her hunch was better than my logic."

"Humph!" grunted the methodical breakfast eater. "What gets me is what came afterward. If anybody'd asked me a week ago if my soon-to-be son-in-law would go out in the woods and pick him three professional thugs and gunfighters, single-handed, and bring 'em in all mussed up and hogtied in their own equipment—"

Barrett laughed. "Your soon-to-be son-in-law might not have been equal to it; I doubt very much if he would. But, you see, a married man has certain responsibilities that can't be shirked. After my wife had led me right up to the jumping-off place, what else was there for me to do? Just think; if I had crawfished then what a life Della might have led me all the way down through the years!"

A grim smile flitted across the granite face of the elderly man.

"The way she tells it, it looks like she tried her prettiest to *make* you crawfish—and you wouldn't. You didn't need to make the fight. You had the money and could have got away with it."

"Oh, well," said Barrett, half embarrassed; "those fellows had it framed up to send me to the pen and I thought it was only fair to give them the same chance they were trying to give me."

"I don't suppose Jimmie ever will admit that he didn't do it just for fun," the young wife broke in. "But if you ever say again that he isn't red-blooded—"

The grizzled fighter of many rude battles of the mining camps grunted his disclaimer.

"I shan't," he agreed. "I ain't aimin' to get myself all tore up and gouged and bit at my time o' life. But, say, Della, baby; it sure does do me a heap o' good to know that you've got you a he-man after all, when it did look so cussedly unlikely a while back. And you can bet on one thing: if them plug-ugly miners up at the 'Little Della' ever get on the rampage again and go to shootin' up the camp I'm going to telegraph for Jimmie to come and put 'em all to bed—I sure am!"

"Well," said Barrett calmly, "I don't know but I might try it. Nothing like keeping your hand in, once you've got it in, you know."

Whereat the young wife laughed and clapped her hands.

"He's called your bluff, daddy!" she crowed. "But please don't wire him until after he has had a little target practice with a six-gun."

A bell-hop came in with a telegram.

"Here is swift action," Barrett commented as he read the typewritten sheet damp from the copying rolls. "I wired President Hawley as soon as we got in and here is his reply:

> "Wire received. Congratulations. Discount all newspaper stories. Nobody here believed you had gone wrong. It was a frame-up, and we have found the stool-pigeon here in the bank. Take a month for your wedding trip instead of two weeks. Respects and all good wishes to Mrs. Barrett. Instructions wired to First National of Copah as to disposition of recovered money. All happiness to you both."

"Fine!" growled the mine owner; and then as the waiter brought covered dishes of hot waffles for two and a piece of apple pie for Barrett: "What's that—pie for breakfast?"

"My mother was a New England woman and I was brought up on pie for breakfast," Barrett explained. Then to the waiter, with a drooping of an eyelid for the young woman opposite: "Please bring me some cheddar cheese; c-h-e-d-d-a-r, cheddar."

And that solemn-faced waiter, mumbling deferentially, "Right, sir," could not understand why the exceedingly pretty young woman sitting across the table from the cheese orderer, suddenly covered her face with her napkin and burst into tears—or laughter; he couldn't decide which.

THE END

Appendix

Notes on Sources

This novel was serialized in four issues of *Argosy* magazine: September 15, September 22, September 29, and October 6 of 1923.

The following text appeared at the opening of each installment:

Author of "A Glorious Fool," "David Vallory," etc.

The following text appeared at the opening of the second installment (no other installment carried a synopsis):

WHAT HAS OCCURRED IN PART I.

JAMES BARRETT, teller in a Denver bank, prepares to go to Ogden for his marriage to the beautiful daughter of a prominent man in the Utah city. President Hawley of the bank asks Barrett to deliver en route at Araquito two hundred thousand dollars in currency required by a client. The president informs his teller that word of the impending money transfer has leaked out into criminal circles, and his belief is that Barrett will not be suspected by the crooks. On the train Barrett takes the treasure valise into the dining car with him. Across the table is a large, fleshy man who winds up his meal with cheddar cheese. Barrett orders black coffee. The next thing to strike his consciousness is the fact that he is a prisoner in a log cabin—and the two hundred thousand dollars is gone. He breaks out, finds himself lost in a remote mountain range, struggles across a strange desert and blindly stumbles into a railroad water tank just in time to escape death from thirst. His obsession is that people will believe he stole the missing money, and he is bitterly determined to track down the robbers and reinstate himself. So he plays hobo on a freight train and inconspicuously enters the city of Copah, where he registers under an assumed name at the best hotel.

Other books available
from the Silver Creek Press

The White Way
A tale of New York's Broadway
by Albert Payson Terhune

The Woman Tamers
Six essays on heart-breakers of history
by Albert Payson Terhune

In Treason's Track
A novel of the American Revolution
by Albert Payson Terhune

The Flood Fighters
A novel first serialized in Country Gentleman
magazine in 1920, published under a
pseudonym and not reprinted until now.
by Albert Payson Terhune

An Albert Payson Terhune Reader

27 stories by Terhune from pulp magazines of the 1910s and 20s,
featuring all original illustrations
by Albert Payson Terhune

Books above and on the previous page are available from the major
bookstores online, as print books and as e-books.

Coming

?? A double novel ??
by Albert Payson Terhune

An Albert Payson Terhune Reader Vol. II

www.ingramcontent.com/pod-product-compliance
Lightning Source LLC
Chambersburg PA
CBHW071839190726
48292CB00005B/1829